Saving Sharlee

Safe and Secure Book 1
USAToday Bestselling Author
Alyssa Bailey

Description

He craved her trust, obedience, and submission in a relationship he knew would never be equal.

Sharlee Armstrong had carefully crafted a safe existence in the shadows of life, trading information for a high price. But when she meets Jacquard Reynaud, she realizes it might be time to take a risk. He's handsome, alluring, and powerful-and Sharlee can't help but be attracted to him, but leaving the safety of her cocoon could be dangerous. Even deadly.

From his first glimpse of her, Jac knows Sharlee must be his-but he also understands getting involved with him could put her in harm's way. Hers is a world of dark exchanges and silent deals, his is a world of pretense and intrigue. Even though they resist the deep attraction they both feel, they work together to forge a working relationship, but it isn't enough. It won't ever be enough. Despite her protests, and his resistance, he finally takes her in hand for her own safety.

Her good name, livelihood, and very life are at risk if she remains with him, but despite his fears, he doesn't have it in him to let her go...for the sake of both their safety. But as they both grow closer to each other, will either of them ever truly be safe?

Love the inside scoop? Sign up for my Newsletter with special offers and bonus content.

https://www.alyssabaileyromance.com

Alyssa Bailey

Saving Becky

Print ISBN: 979-8-9871524-4-7

Cover Design by Joe Dugdale

Prologue

C harlotte strode confidently out of the building that held the offices of Reynaud & Associates. Clients and employees referred to them as Jac's Group. Their job was to keep their clients safe and secure. That mandate included at home, in the office, or out in the world. Jac's operatives were the best of the best, and anyone who needed to know that did.

This was why she was in this building, officially on the Alpha team, but working for the entire group. She was numbered as one of the best worldwide in cyber security protocol. The power she held in her hand for her clients, both privately and as part of Jac's Group was mindboggling. And she loved it. Remaining in control of her life was her superpower.

She remembered the first time she'd entered the building with much less confidence. They had approached her at a time when she felt restless and took a look at what the security team was offering. Her skills weren't in question, but her ability to be in the world was daunting. Part of her success and continuing safety was her ability to stay under the radar.

She'd always preferred to work at home, alone. She chose specific contracts for a variety of reasons, one being she didn't conform well to other's rules. The other reason was her clients weren't interested in meeting her face to face, in fact, preferred not to. All she needed to work with was a legitimate bank account and her business set up. She remained shadowy as Vaper. It was rare that someone knew her actual IRS name. Indeed, her line of work relied on her ability to remain anonymous.

Her fees were steep and only a very select, highly vetted group of clients could afford her. They called often, sometimes too often. She'd been perfectly happy doing that exclusively until Jacquard Reynaud approached her.

Charlotte had just finished an intense contract and was looking forward to a break when the call came in, asking if she'd be interested in working for their company on a more permanent basis. Over the phone, she'd thought they were just fishing, but when they set up an interview, she was curious. The timing was perfect: she was ripe for some adventure and possibly a holiday, so she agreed to a meeting, not expecting much to come of it.

Flying in to see what they had to offer, Charlotte didn't expect that she'd be as interested as they said she'd be. She was wrong. The interview was one she'd never forget. Jacquard Reynaud had picked her up from the airport, and since she had researched him, he was easy to spot. He had almost coal black hair. She imagined it would shimmer blue in a certain light, but she couldn't determine his nationality. His skin had warm undertones that made his tan even richer. His eyes were just this side of black as well.

Seems he had done the same internet check on her, but less thorough. "Miss Armstrong?"

"Please, call me Charlotte."

"And I'm Jac."

"Yes, I recognize you from your pictures. You're the only one I've found with that name easy to research, not that there was much out there. Good for you, but it means I need to ask more questions." Charlotte decided not to tell him that the group, including him was easily found and identified on a deeper net profile. Not yet anyway. Most would never go further than the surface.

Jac grimaced and then turned to usher her to the baggage claim. "Thank God. Most people have no idea what my real name is and usually assume the company has something to do with clothing or fabric. The name was a gift from my father, who loved it and pronounced it in the soft French way. Dad may be French, but my mother is Shawnee, Kentucky, born and bred. I aspire to be a lover like the French, romantic and spontaneous, but from Mom I get my tougher, more pragmatic nature. The two cultures made for an interesting childhood. She pronounces my name with a K sound, making it sound harsh, but has only ever called me Jac. There, all you ever wanted to know about that odd name is now in your trivia file."

"And now I also know where your coloring comes from, your mother, and why you picked here to set up business,."

He chuckled. "I guess so, in part, anyway. You're fast at putting the puzzle pieces together. I like that."

"Thanks, but that was easy. I can do much more with a computer."

"Actually, I picked Lexington because I could be close to contacts and contracts, but not too close. And I love horses like my father. He and mom have just retired from here to Florida. I enjoy a good race as well."

At the baggage claim, he looked at the bags and waved his arm. "Which one is yours?"

"Bag? Oh, I travel light." She held up her small roller bag. "This is it."

He gave her a confused look. "Then why are we here?"

"I don't know. I just followed you," said Charlotte with a laugh.

His slow, sheepish smile seemed contrary to the powerful businessman persona, but it made Charlotte's heart pump a little faster. Jac Reynaud was a handsome man. "Okay, then. Let's get out of here." The pressure of his hand, radiating heat into the small of her back, sent a shiver up her spine. "Lets get you out of here and into a warm car." Considerate and watchful, two things that could be trouble if she was offered and accepted the job.

"Sounds good. I haven't picked a hotel yet, so if you could find me one close to the—"

It felt like a freight train had just hit her. Did she step into the airport traffic lane by accident? As she was orienting herself on the ground, Jac leaned down.

"Charlotte, are you okay?"

Embarrassed, she said, "Yes. Fine."

"Be right back."

Jac threw his keys in her direction, landing neatly in her lap, and took off in hot pursuit of what, she wasn't sure. Maybe coming out of her roomy apartment in an undisclosed location was not a good idea.

A woman tried to help Charlotte up but already leery of the humans around her, she politely but brusquely declined. By the time she was upright again, and had brushed off her casual clothes, all she ever wore, Charlotte walked over to a seat, pulling her case behind her, and sat to wait for Jac to reappear.

What else was she supposed to do? Feeling out of place and drawing attention was something Charlotte hated.

After another few moments, Jac came strolling back down the sidewalk alongside an officer and a man in handcuffs. She was relieved to see him and then irritated that he had left her. Jac approached her and immediately placed his hand on her left bicep, taking an appraising look before squatting down in front of her on the metal bench. He spoke. His voice was concerned, tender, which put her belly into acrobatics and her core radiating a pulsing heat throughout her lower regions. This man.

"You good, Charlotte? Are you hurt anywhere?"

"A little shaken up, but nothing I can't recover from." She tried to laugh off the shaky feeling she had.

"That's my girl. You will tell me if that changes." Again, not a question. "I'll take you to drop your bag and then we'll get some breakfast right after I finish this business. Shouldn't be too much longer. No one should get away with a snatch and run, especially involving an elderly woman. And then, he knocks you over." He shook his head. "I haven't seen one of those in town. D.C., sure, but here? Nah."

He stood and moved his hand to her shoulder and held it there as though he thought Charlotte was going to take off or he was being protective. That last thought sent another uncontrollable shiver through her. Maybe she should have stayed home. Her devil on the other shoulder said, *What, and miss this? No way. Most action I've had all year. No, make that several years.*

About fifteen minutes later, Jac led her to his nice, fancy car. She didn't know much about cars, but she was willing to count on this one being expensive. They didn't say much on the way to the hotel. Jac left her in a room his assistant had secured for her, right across the street from his office.

"I have about an hour's worth of work I have to do, but then I'll call you and pick you up outside. Is that enough time to rest a little before dinner?"

"Um, sure."

Jac nodded, and after escorting her to her room and then checking it to make sure she was alone, he strolled out. "I'll be back in an hour."

What a welcome to the city of Lexington, Kentucky.

Dinner was relaxing and fun. She met Garrett briefly, as he had a date at the same restaurant. They introduced the woman as Callie and Charlotte got the impression they were more than dating but, her people skills were less honed than her computer skills. Jac had an easy, polished manner that switched to professional when he was greeted by clients, which happened a handful of times during the course of one dinner. He always introduced her as Charlotte, a business colleague, and left it at that. Curiosity met that vagueness of identity from the men and thinly veiled hostility from the women.

Jac walked her to her hotel door. "I'll just check your room and then leave you for the evening."

"You don't have to do that. I'm not concerned."

"You should be. Personal safety is important. You'll let me check."

It wasn't a question, and that confidence frustrated and aroused her. She stepped aside and waved him in. She imagined not much could stop the man if he was intent on doing something he believed in. And she might not have had much in-person social life, but she knew this man was intense and could really do a number on her libido if she let him. And yet, no freaking way was she going to allow anyone to take control of her libido or anything else. That is when life got dangerous.

"All good. I'll see you at nine in the morning. We will provide breakfast. Anything you are allergic to?" Jac hesitated for a couple of seconds and Charlotte thought he was going to say something else, but he didn't.

"Not that I know of. I'll see you then, and thanks for dinner."

"The least I could do after your rude greeting at the airport. I promise to ensure that is all the excitement during this trip, unless you endorse it."

"Thank you?"

Jac hesitated again before saying, "I'll get going, then. Lock this door with all the locks."

"I'll be fine."

"Charlotte."

Was that his chastising tone and why the hell was she wanting to squeeze her thighs together? Oh, he was serious alright.

"I will. See you in the morning."

"Night." He stepped out of the doorway and damn if he didn't stand on the other side of the door and wait for her to lock the door. Was he for real? And were there others like him?

She made a show of turning the locks loudly. "And the top latch." She did. His footfalls could be heard down the hall to the elevator. Shouldn't she be more upset about that behavior? Yes, she should be.

Charlotte had rarely been up at nine in the morning, so she was glad she didn't have a contract she was working, or she'd have been up late. She took a leisurely bath, watched a movie, and checked her nightly webpages before reading a few chapters of a hot, dominant man, sassy woman romance and finishing her evening with a vibrator induced orgasm while thinking of Jac in the dom role of her book. She came hard.

The next morning, bright and still too early, Charlotte arrived with her computer bag and a cup of coffee, her second of the morning. She wasn't usually up for breakfast, so this was another first. This trip was full of them so far.

She spent the rest of the day interviewing, explaining what she knew about their company and asking questions in between theirs. It took most of the day and it was clear by the end of it that these men meant to find the best. Well, she was the best. Digging into who they were as people, their mission statement impressed Charlotte, their ethics and moral guidelines for their lives and their business, and their expectations for the company.

She expected working with them would give her the diversity that she was lacking. They had VIP clients, domestic and international. They worked for anyone who met their boundary lines and stayed within them. All marks in their favor. Anything she did with this business would be with clients that she wouldn't have to scrutinize as much to make sura e she was on the right side of the law. Heaven knew the government had to be monitored when she worked for them.

Charlotte still didn't know if she had won the contract, so she would wait them out. Jac had more to this interview.

"There are several teams, but this is the one you would I would assign you to and the one that will use you the most, as their assignments involve more than bodyguarding, putting up safety cameras and monitoring those set ups. There are some

VIP jobs that we might need some help with, research mostly, but then I need backgrounds and cyber work done for more delicate jobs."

"Okay, that didn't sound vague at all."

His partners Garrett and Monroe smiled as well as the other members of the Alpha team, Mark, Kaden, and Carter. Rebecca was his assistant, and she seemed to know everything. Finally, their lawyer, Ryker, was personable but restrained.

Garrett and Monroe were hard to read. One minute they seemed to be polar opposites, the next they were saying the same sentences. It might take a while to tease the differences out, but that was half the fun. For now, Garrett was the brown-haired man with the striking violet-blue eyes that could become animated when he was debating an issue. Monroe had light hair and icy blue eyes that were surprisingly less chilly than the color would have implied.

Then there were Mark and Carter. Mark was dark: hair, eyes, and personality, for that matter. Carter? Well, Carter's huge stature hid a kind and gentle nature unless, by his own admission, he was hungry.

"If I'm hungry, I get irritated. Then you head for higher ground." A grin that warmed the whole room followed this declaration.

Kaden came over and sat down next to her. This man was more open than the others and probably nearer to her age, too. He seemed hardware savvy and would be her equipment go-to person if she decided to work with them. She expected him to be easier to talk to than the others.

"Except for Kaden, you all have last names as first names. Did you notice that? Sorry, I tend to notice patterns in things."

"Nope, but we didn't notice we were all over the internet in bits and pieces until we had an expert scrub all but the most innocuous information from public view, either. Amazing what you can share even when you aren't meaning to."

"Keeps me in business," said Charlotte.

"Right, well, we're hired for a large assortment of jobs, but analyzing threats and eliminating them is the long and the short of it."

"Is it legal?"

Monroe answered. "The job we are trying to fill is legal."

Charlotte hesitated before responding. "I sense a 'but' in there."

"Nope," said Kaden.

"Good, because I'm not going to be part of anything shady. I mean, working on government contracts is too close for comfort sometimes." Charlotte unsuccessfully suppressed a shiver when she thought of her last job. Things had gotten very dicey at the end before she zipped things up and got out of the mess. She wasn't about to clean up their cyber fallout.

"What was that thought?" asked Jac.

"What? Oh, nothing too wild. Just remembering my last government job."

"Does working with the government bother you because we do that, too? Usually it is for the government through a person, though."

"That is how they work in my world too, but sometimes it's better to get in, get the job done, and get out fast, making sure you close the door quietly behind you."

Mark spoke for the first time. "We don't operate like those morons and besides, we do private contracts, not government ones, meaning private people hire us, not governments."

"Right. So what do you want me to do? Specifically. How would I enhance your work?"

"We really need a good techie, one who can do the job without setting off alarms. Our contracts are so broad that we need a diverse person. We've run through some scenarios with you, but I get the feeling you're concerned about something."

"I am. There've been so many undefined companies springing up that are, frankly, all below the water level and some are just dipping there. Others, the totally above-board ones, are very specialized. And, for the record, I'm not a *techie*. I'm a Cyber Security Expert."

Jac nodded. "The best of the best, we hear."

"I'm up in the top five, anyway."

They'd chatted through lunch and finally went to a late dinner. When Jac finally returned her to her hotel, he offered her a drink in the hotel bar. Charlotte agreed and met him in the bar twenty minutes later. They sat in silence, enjoying their chosen beverages—Jac chose a Highland whisky and Charlotte picked a white wine—contemplating the situation and each other.

"So here's the thing, Charlotte, we work on highly sensitive contracts. Contracts the assorted government and state agencies would take on if they could, but for one reason or another, they either can't or won't. We do anything from finding a missing person, to vetting people on a guest list, to ensuring an attorney makes it to court every day on a high-profile case."

"I see. And I would be support for those contracts."

"Yes, and no. Yes, in that you would support us, but we have support people to do the low-grade things. You would be an integral part of the team. We would need to trust each other implicitly."

"I normally work alone and in my apartment."

"Unfortunately, that isn't negotiable. We're a team and the only way to stay bonded is to physically work together, often. Not that you can't work at home on some things. In fact, you'll probably need a well thought out set-up there as well, but it'll have to be in this town or near enough to it to get to the office."

"I'm sorry, Jac. I can't agree to do a nine-to-five job because I don't do that kind of work."

"I understand. None of us do, but we all live within twenty miles. Look, it's getting late," said Jac. "I'd like to stop by tomorrow morning, take you to breakfast before you leave on your afternoon flight. Answer any other questions you might have and ask any that I might think up later tonight."

"I'd like that."

Three months later, she was working in her new office at Reynaud & Associates. During that three-month transition, she had sublet her apartment, rented a good-sized apartment within twenty minutes of the business, thanks to Rebecca. She had reassembled her system with even more bells and whistles than she had previously, thanks to Jac.

The company's technology was in its infancy stage, much more so than any of their personal security gear, which was high tech. Charlotte settled in to setting up what she knew they'd need. The challenge was just the change she was looking for and collaborating with the guys, as she affectionately called them, wasn't as difficult as it had first seemed.

Rebecca, or Becky as she begged Charlotte to call her, seemed to be the one with her finger on the pulse of the business and Charlotte enjoyed talking to her. Becky not only answered her questions, but she also filled a gap Charlotte hadn't realized was there before moving. Charlotte hadn't had many friends since joining the adult world that she could take a coffee break in person with, so this was a treat. Becky seemed to love it, too.

Charlotte looked at the building she had just exited and smiled. She had taken the chance to change her life for the better. Now, months after she had answered the invitation to talk, she was part of this kick-ass team, and she was happy with her choice. Well, except she had a crush on her new boss.

Jacquard Reynaud was exotic to look at, intense to work with, and easy to trust. She was excited to get to know him better. No girlfriend. She got the impression that the only one with a steady girlfriend might be Garrett. They were typical men, not ready to settle down. She wasn't either.

And she certainly didn't need to have an affair with her boss. But a girl could dream, even if the reality was an affair would inevitably end, and the mess at work would be unbearable. No, she would look but not touch and learn to be satisfied with him visiting her dreams. It would have to be enough.

Chapter 1

"Hey, Charlie, want some coffee?" Charlotte looked up to see Kaden smiling and waving a coffee pot in the air.

"Yes, thanks, but don't call me Charlie."

"Sorry, but Charlotte isn't going to last around here. I mean, Rebecca at reception is fine as Rebecca, but our team isn't going to handle Charlotte for long. Charlie is a good compromise to Char or Lottie."

They both cringed at those. "Actually, I don't like Charlie, and Rebecca prefers Becky."

"Really? I'll have to share that bit of information. Now, back to you. I'm serious here. Before someone assigns something more hideous, let's agree on Charlie."

"How about Sharl—"

"Charlie? When did we start calling you Charlie? It's about time. Charlotte is so formal," declared Monroe, as he grabbed the pot from Kaden.

"Well, I didn't agree."

Carter walked in with Garrett. "Hey," called out Monroe, "we can call her Charlie now."

"Good. Jac said we couldn't push her on something like that. I mean, she can be called anything she wants, but Charlie just works better," replied Carter.

"Um..."

Garrett walked up behind her. His voice was quietly firm. "Do you want me to tell them to knock it off? If you want to be called only Charlotte, you have to speak up now."

She looked at him ruefully. "Well, I guess I can get used to it, but I prefer Sharlee."

"Gotcha, but you need to learn to hold your own with these guys. They have to learn to trust your word and if you just let them get away with little things like this, they won't know whether to believe you or not about the big things. Think about it." He patted her hand and walked away. Well, shoot. He definitely had a point. Later that day, Jac came in and corrected Kaden when he called her Charlie.

"No, Jac, it's cool. She's okay with it."

Jac looked at her and raised his eyebrow almost to a point over his left eye. She simply smiled wryly and shrugged her shoulders as if to say, "It's not worth the fight."

Jac walked closer to her. "You good with this, really?"

"It's fine. I shouldn't be so touchy."

"Charlotte, it's your name."

"I know. I prefer Sharlee if I must have it shortened, but I've decided the guys can call me Charlie if they are more comfortable with it, but no other derivatives."

Jac nodded and whistled loudly. "Listen up, you morons. Charlotte prefers her given name, but if you must shorten it, it is Sharlee, not Charlie. Do I need to spell it, or can you handle it?" There were murmurs around the room and then agreement that it wasn't a half bad compromise.

From then on, the only one to call her Charlotte consistently was Jac, the man who visited her regularly in her dreams.

TODAY'S LONG DAY HAD turned into tonight's long night. She had to do just a little bit more. She was used to pushing herself, but not used to others noticing or caring.

"Charlotte, it's time to go home." Jac reached for the papers on her desk.

"What? No, I have so much more to do." Charlotte scrambled for her reference material and tried to push him away.

"Tomorrow is another day, and I will not have you getting rundown and sick because you over worked yourself. You don't have to prove anything." She grabbed at her stack of papers, still in Jac's hand, currently being held out of her reach.

"I know I don't, but I'm not a two-year-old. I know all about tomorrow. It's the day I won't be able to see above the pile of work I have if I don't stay and do more tonight."

"If you don't act like a toddler, you won't be treated like one."

Sharlee tried to ignore him. She looked at her screen, diverted from the conversation by another tidbit that caught her interest.

"Charlotte Hope Armstrong shut it down, now."

Her tummy wiggled in arousal, but she was too busy to stop and do more than acknowledge both her dampening panties and her demanding boss. "Argh. Would you just go home? I know how to lock up."

"It's eight o'clock. I'm going to close up my office and so are you. If I come back and you haven't done as instructed, there will be consequences. Am I understood?"

"Okay, okay." She sounded like she was whining at being denied her treat, and yet, she almost wanted to know what the consequences would be like. Almost. One day, she would push that magic button and see what happened. But she was too tired tonight.

SHE HAD OFFICIALLY invaded his dreams. Charlotte was never off his mind for long, and it was driving him crazy. She was incredibly intelligent. He liked everything about her, from her well-proportioned body to her sharp wit. She could easily become buried in a task and have to be literally taken away, like he had just done.

She agreed reluctantly, but Jac saw that antsy wiggle and wondered if it was because his small show of dominance flipped her switch or because she really was too preoccupied to listen. He left her with no doubt that he was serious. If she were his, she'd already be sporting a blush from her first taste of a hot bottom. If she persisted, she'd have the full-on sizzle, the result of his hard hand kissing her gorgeous jiggling ass.

Jac was a virile man in his late thirties who enjoyed spanking his women for both fun and discipline. His previous partners had all been more experienced than he was sure Charlotte was and that is what he typically looked for, but none had been long-term choices. As he thought about Charlotte, he accepted he hadn't felt this strongly for a woman in a long time, maybe ever.

Hell, she wasn't even thirty, and she was his employee. Jac caught her looking at him with something in her green eyes, but he wasn't pursuing. He should recalibrate his sights, but he didn't know if he could. He needed to be sure she was prepared for what he had to offer first. She might never be. And that would suck.

Walking back out, he saw she had packaged up her things but was still sitting and looking at her screen. The little minx was doing her best to get a hot backside, and he was going to try his best not to give it to her. The boundaries were clear, but damn if he didn't want her and the way he wanted her was decadent.

"Charlotte, are you looking for a spanking?"

"What?" she sputtered as she quickly shifted from looking at the screen to looking at Jac as her face turned deep red. She must have decided it was a serious question. "Um, no sir, I was just waiting for you."

She hit a few keys, turned off her monitor, and walked toward the elevators. He reached behind her and swatted her ass once, hard, on his way to turn off the lights. He made sure she understood the smack as the warning it was meant to be.

"Ow," she said in response as she scooted out of his path and turned her bottom away from him at the elevator. She wasn't outraged and almost sounded as though she had expected it.

"Do not disobey a direct order and don't be slow in your compliance of the same."

His tone was firm as he watched her intently. She nodded. It appeared as though she was fighting the urge to rub the smacked cheek. She was biting her lip. Could that swat have turned the little minx on? No, he was reading more into it than was there. He wouldn't pursue. Couldn't pursue, but he damn sure wanted to pick her up and toss her over his shoulder like the Neanderthal she often called the guys.

Jac was glad Charlotte was backed away and averted her eyes because his increasingly hardening cock would have been obvious otherwise. He was relieved when the elevator swished open.

They reached the garage and Jac walked her to her car, and said, "You pull out ahead of me and once I see you're out, I'll follow." Then he watched as she started her car and pulled out. There were only a few cars in the garage and the disobedient minx waited for him to do the same before preceding him out to the street. It was a nice gesture, and he was sure she thought she was keeping him safe as well. He would never point out that he would be less distracted in a dangerous situation if she were not in the vicinity of the same danger. He shook his head.

The image of Sharlee's reaction to his swat followed him into his dreams and he was up at four just to give attention to his perpetual hard on. Jac found his relief while thinking of Charlotte willingly taking his discipline, followed by hot, paint peeling sex. He rolled over and thought about how screwed he was. He had it bad for her. No other woman had even come close to arousing him since Sharlee arrived.

He'd been off the dating circuit for about six months before Charlotte signed on, but since she joined the team, she was the only one in his bedroom scenes. Maybe he just needed to get laid, but as soon as that thought entered his head, he saw Charlotte under him, riding him, presenting her ass for him. Still unable to sleep despite the stress relief, he admitted defeat. He might as well get his run out of the way.

Walking into the office, Jac was jazzed. His early start to the day made him feel as though he had the tiger by the tail. He breezed through the next few meetings. He ordered lunch in so the team could huddle on the next stage of their newest contract. Charlotte was moody. She had been working on the face recognition program she'd collaborated on during grad school over five years ago and still wasn't satisfied.

It was still nearly the best out there, and that was a hell of a lot more than they had without her. They didn't sell the patent or make the program public. Only Charlotte and two others had the rights to use it and only one other had continued in the direction where that program was beneficial.

She'd tweaked the facial recognition program even further, fine-tuning it using her nearly unfettered access to government programs, which she retained because of the occasional side job she still accepted from them. Those contracts were outside Jac's team, and he didn't like it. However, business was benefiting, so unless it became a problem for Charlotte performing her work for the teams, he said nothing. It was a symbiotic relationship just like Charlotte and Jac's as yet unnamed personal affiliation.

Charlotte closed her office door much harder than required. It seemed to startle her, and she stood outside it as though deciding what to do. Monroe came to the rescue.

"Sharlee, you okay? Something upset you?"

"Yes." She shook her head. "No, I mean, I didn't mean for it to close so hard."

"Maybe you need to take a walk around the building," suggested Monroe.

"That's a good idea. I'll be back in a bit."

She turned to open her door again and turned the handle several times in frustration.

"Sharlee, you need to—"

Jac stepped in. "Charlotte, walk with me before you force me to help you refocus." She wiggled and looked down. "No, look at me." When she didn't, he got stern. Leaning down, he placed his hand on the small of her back. "You are too frustrated or irritated or something. Time to go for a walk."

"I was going back to get my wallet and do that."

"No need. I'll cover your coffee and snack."

"How did you..."

"It's my business to be observant and those I care about, those in my created family. They are top of the list as far as significance goes. Of course, I'm going to pay attention that you get moody at three every afternoon on the days you skip lunch. I have to just wait and see what happens at three to know if you worked through lunch or not. Now, walk with me."

Sharlee sighed and nodded agreement. "I didn't mean to miss lunch. I was actually hungry, but I needed to run one more scenario before stopping, and that turned into several hours."

"Do I need to set an alarm and make sure you leave the office at noon?"

"What? Absolutely not. I just don't work well in an office environment. I work on my own schedule. This is just harder than I thought it would be."

"What day can I give you to work at home?"

"You'd do that?"

"Sure. If it works out, we can expand that, but we are still getting to know you and it's important for you to be here."

"Is it really, because no one else is in the office much."

"But their job is out in the community. Yours is here, performing your magic. I can't believe how we ever survived or got jobs without you." He wondered how he'd ever done without her, either.

"Thanks." She ordered a large coffee with lots of cream and sugar and a huge Bear Claw pastry.

"A large coffee, please, and I'll share her bear claw."

"No, you won't." She looked at the woman. "He needs his own."

Jac laughed. "I love that have no trouble asking for what you want. Nothing behind the veil with you."

She smiled and then dropped it quickly and shrugged. That said, more to him than her words. His newest employee had a secret or two hidden away. He'd have to work on that later, but right now, he was going to sit and watch her eat her too much sugar, too much yeast, too much of so many things pastry and try not to hear her sounds of enjoyment while telling his cock to stand down.

He wanted to scold her for substituting a healthy lunch with this, but he didn't have the heart to stop her enjoyment.

She stopped and looked at him pensively. "Friday."

"Excuse me?"

"Friday. That's the day I want to work at home. I'd like Monday, too, but I guess that would be pushing it too far, huh?" She licked some icing off her fingers, and he nearly groaned. He wanted her so badly that if he sat her any longer, he'd embarrass himself. He stood up abruptly.

"Friday is fine." At least he'd get some work accomplished.

"Wait, I'm not done, and you haven't even tasted yours. I promise they are so good." There went her tongue again. This time she exaggerated your sounds of enjoyment.

"Have mine. I have a meeting in a few minutes."

She looked disappointed. A small price to pay to keep his dignity.

How would you feel if I told you how much I craved you? How could she not know how much I want that sweet tongue in my mouth, then on my cock? Where I want to put my tongue? Spank that ass when you are sassy.

Yeah, he wasn't about to rock that boat either.

Chapter 2

It had been another long but productive week with two contracts closed and one private contracted completed. Another week of men that were possessive and overprotective at times, but it was the best Sharlee had ever felt since leaving home as a new college student. Actually, while she'd always been well cared for, that male protectiveness went missing when her dad was killed in an auto accident. She was eight when she lost him. For once, she was glad it was nearly time to knock off. She needed a diversion.

It was her week to stay until closing, meaning no Friday at home this week. In fact, that had only worked out one out of three weeks. It was better than nothing. The guys didn't like that she insisted on being on the closing roster, but she had insisted and finally Jac agreed but demanded she be out by six-thirty. They were so protective they would be uncontainable if they knew she was about to go on a little hunting expedition alone. Her tummy twinged.

The work was sometimes difficult to deal with, especially when they were trying to expose creeps for what they were on someone else's nickel, but it was worth it. The Alpha team didn't do bodyguard work for just anyone, but sometimes, under certain circumstances, they did what they needed to do to accomplish the task. Whatever was necessary. She often made a difference she could see. She hoped today would be one of those times.

As Charlotte was shutting things down and clearing the office of the last support workers, she decided to follow the lead she had discovered on her own. She cringed at her own thought. Jac, Garrett, really all the guys had made it abundantly clear that going rogue or off the grid without authorization was frowned upon. And she was never allowed to do anything alone. It was a safety issue.

She understood that. She did. But honestly, it wasn't that big a deal. She just was going to check out the lead to see if it would uncover anything she should share. It wasn't dangerous, but it meant going off the grid just a little. Doing it in the evening meant she didn't have to tell anyone and therefore could avoid the scolding these men, who had become more like older, bossy brothers, did frequently. And since she and Becky were the only women the guys had daily contact with; they received the brunt of that unsolicited protective attention.

Before she could second guess her decision, Sharlee jumped in the car, locked the door, and headed twenty miles into the country. The drive away from the second half of rush hour traffic was nice, and she rolled down the window partway to enjoy the balmy early spring breeze.

Turning onto the appropriate road, she craned her neck to look for a house that, while it had an address, she couldn't find on satellite pictures of the area. Those photos were several years old, and it might be a new building. Her belly rumbled a little. Shoot, she should have brought something to munch on. She liked going places with Carter because he always had a stash. The guys were catching on and putting healthy snacks in their vehicles and desks. Granola was good, but some cake would have been better.

Sharlee had been monitoring a suspicious group of communications and had tracked the signal to this house. She knew her hunch might be all washed up, but it was odd not to have any map point. Maybe there wasn't a road to it even though it gave a street address. The light was beginning to wane, and soon the sun would set. Charlotte considered turning back, but told herself she could push on just a little further. If she found nothing, it would satisfy her need to know tonight. She could come back tomorrow and have a better search if need be.

Looking at the stills she had of the coordinates, she didn't see a house anywhere. Discouraged, she turned onto a small dirt side road that looked like it was the way to get to the nonexistent house and when she saw nothing decided to turn around and go home. As she made a loop to roll into a U-turn, she heard a popping sound followed by a 'poof' and her car sank slightly. Damn, a flat tire. When she got out to identify which one to change, she was irritated that there were two flats. One flat she could handle, but two was more than she had replacement tires for and plenty odd.

Looking to see what was on the road that could have caused the blowouts, she found a small bit of wood with nails on it. If she had been going faster, she'd have blown all four tires. Angry that she'd need a tow truck, she glanced around the surrounding area for the first time. She'd known it was a little off the grid, but now, with the sun low in the sky, it was creepier than she bargained for, and she needed help.

Luckily, another one of those billboard signs advertising a towing company that she had been passing was right in front of her. She figured the guy must live nearby. The light was changing faster than she had imagined it would, indicating the sun would soon set, and she would be out here, off the road, in the dark. Alone. Her thoughts ran to Jac, but she was a grown woman who could handle this. Sharlee dialed the number, and in less than ten minutes, a truck drove up. She relaxed. Good, soon she'd have her tires changed and be back on the road headed home with no one the wiser.

"Looks like you're in a bit of a bind, miss."

Sharlee looked at the man and hesitated before speaking. "I guess I am. I think I ran over something because both of my front tires are blown. It's just my luck." She decided to keep her find to herself. Something was off, but she wasn't sure if it was her paranoia or what. It was odd that in the place she thought was under the radar activity, she had both tires blown. Too coincidental. "Obviously, I only have one spare tire. Could you get me to the nearest gas station?"

"Sure, but I have a shop about half a mile further down this road. I could fix you up in no time."

The man reached for a metal hook to attach to the under the casing of her car without saying another word. Charlotte jumped from behind her car door where she had been standing.

"Hey, wait. Don't do that."

He walked up closer to Sharlee, causing her stomach to revolt from the bad vibes she got. *Don't show your fear,* she told herself as the odious man positively leered at her, causing her body to seize with anxiety. His dirty shirt declared there was 'No such thing as bad sex.' Her panic rose. She needed Jac or Garrett or any of the guys.

"What's wrong? Don't you want help?" The man seemed to ooze the sleaze factor.

"Well, um, do you take credit cards?"

His smile was lewd. "Sorry, little lady, I only accept cash."

Speaking through her fear, she said, "Your truck says you take credit cards."

Then the creepy man sneered and said he could only accept cash after dark. "But we could work it out if you like." His grin revealed a set of dingy yellow teeth that made the acid in her stomach roil.

She looked at the ever-darkening sky as she contemplated his words. "That doesn't make... Just a moment," she said. "Don't hook me anymore until I see if I can get the cash."

God, something was terribly wrong, and it felt like a crappy but equally horrifying version of the Bates Motel. She jumped back into her car, locked the door, and called Jac. He made her stay on the line while every available man was called to show up in response to her mayday call. She was privy to his choice of words about the situation as he made the calls while she was on the phone. She cringed. He was royally pissed at her. She was in so much trouble, but he gentled his voice after she heard Garrett tell him to calm her, not make her cry. She gave a wobbly smile. He was a good guy.

"Charlotte, honey, listen to me. I want you to stay safe in your car and do not get out of it. Do not get out."

"But Jac, he could hook me up and..." she heard the pathetic sob she couldn't hide.

"Baby, listen. There isn't any place he can take you that I can't find you. Stay in your car."

"Okay." She turned to the man lounging at the front of her car. "I just called my friend to bring me some cash," she said through the small opening at the top of her window.

She made sure it was small enough that he could not get his fingers inside while she sat and bounced her leg nervously.

"Got another gal bringing money, huh? I'll wait in the truck." He rubbed his hands as though she had ordered him a seven-course meal.

Charlotte would have laughed when the guys showed up if her relief wasn't so profound. The tow truck man was understandably worried when two large black SUVs and six brawny men poured out, swarming the scene like bees to the honeycomb. Garrett, Monroe, Mark, Carter, and Kaden stood between her and the truck, assessing the situation. Jac asked the driver if he took a credit card and the driver answered in the affirmative.

"Dumb fuck," was Jacquard's reply just before Carter sent his fisted hand into the man's jaw.

Then the police showed up because they had called them, not because they needed them, but because they needed to keep things legal. This time. Then the questioning began. The board was located and pulled out of the grass and uncovered from its resting spot on the barely carved-out road. When that was all cleared up, and the police had arrested him for a variety of evidently illegal things, Charlotte got into the back seat of the SUV with Jac, as ordered.

"What about my car?"

Sharlee couldn't believe how submissive she felt right now. Cared for, but also how an errant child must feel like when she was found to be doing something she knew was wrong.

"The guys will take care of your car. We'll get you home. What were you doing out here? And Charlotte, tell the whole truth."

"I needed to check something out."

"Damn, sweetheart, what was going on in your mind to go off the main road in the dark and then call a complete stranger to help you when you have any number of knuckleheads ready to defend your honor and rescue you?"

"What? How was I to know that you couldn't trust a tow guy? I mean, aren't they bonded?"

"I'm sure they are, but why didn't you call one of us to come and take care of the issue?"

Jac listened quietly, but Charlotte wasn't so shaken that she didn't notice his left hand flexing open and closed. She'd seen that before and Becky said that's his spanking hand. He's a right-handed person with a left-handed dribble and spanking hand. Monroe drove, also remaining quiet while she spoke. She was exhausted, and her voice gave her away.

Sharlee ignored his question. "Jac, something else is going on there. I know it. I've intercepted communications on the dark web that connects to operations that land here, to a place close to where we just were. They have been tracked on Onion."

"Onion?"

"It's a route that contains information passage through Tor. Governments like using it because you can't track information. Usually. Once you are in Tor, you can't track well, but going in and coming out you can. That is where I've picked up some information to follow."

"And you didn't think to tell me?"

"I wanted to prove I could do things on my own."

"Prove to whom because I distinctly remember getting intel on you that said if I could snag you, I would never be behind world events, or changing technology, and I would have my finger on the pulse of all that matters. Are you not still that woman?"

"Yes, but I'm used to doing something about things in the world. I can orchestrate whole countries' financial futures with a few clicks of my keyboard. I make it possible for countries to meet in their own languages in their own countries via the web while staying almost completely untraceable. But here? I'm not part of the team. I'm helpful, but that's it." Jac's hand rifled through his hair in obvious frustration.

"And so again, why would you come out here, at night, alone? We all need backup."

"Jac, I can handle things on my own." She sounded whiny even to her own ears.

"Right, as this proved so well. You don't need to handle things like this while any of us is available. Don't make that mistake again, understood?"

"Sure, whatever," was her response, accompanied by a huff and a shrug. It was the wrong response.

"Right, I thought we could deal with this differently, but I'm not happy with not doing it my way, and you're obviously not happy handling it this way either, so over you go."

"What?"

"Over my lap, sweetheart."

Sharlee tried to backpedal. "No... I... okay wait. I guess I thought since I was off duty, it was my problem."

Monroe whistled and shook his head while looking at her in the rear-view mirror, but said nothing.

"You signed the paperwork. It said you would notify one of us when there was a problem."

"With work, Jac. This wasn't for work. Well, it is really, but it's after hours."

"With anything, Charlotte Hope, you should know that."

"Why would I know that?"

"Because it was in the paperwork, and we have done so much to show you we mean business. Safety is our game and you and Becky, along with any of the support staff, are ours to protect. You and Becky, all day, every day. You two are part of the team."

She fell silent. What else could she say? Not that she loved the feeling of having all these guys watch out for her like her newly acquired brothers. Certainly not that she had a crush on her boss and, for the first time in her life, wanted to really impress someone. Her short soiree into power exchange play with her last lover, that lasted about a month, had lit her every burning need to go deeper.

Jac had to be eight years her senior, at least, but he was the hottest specimen she had seen, possibly ever. And under no circumstances would she tell him that she was a closet spank lover that had never gotten anyone to care enough about her to actually spank her. Not. One. Lover. Nor would she tell him that she masturbated to the time he had swatted her ass at the elevator.

She murmured like a repentant child. "I'm sorry. I didn't realize it meant outside of work as well. But why?"

"Why what?"

"Why worry when I'm not working?"

"Look, Sharlee, you are still relatively new to the idea, but—"

"I've been here six months, long enough to figure things out."

"And some of us have been together for over a decade. As I was saying," he gave her a hard stare, "We worked hard putting this team together. Garrett and I, and later Monroe, vetted every single one of you for a time before we signed you on. We have support people to keep us going, but when we went looking for a member of the team who could cover all the computer work, we had expected the best would be a man."

She opened her mouth in surprise, and he shrugged unashamedly. "Sorry, but that's how it was. We never expected a woman on the team. Hadn't even considered it, but we found you touted to be one of the best in the field, and we reluctantly interviewed you. You impressed the hell out of us, and we all knew we had to have you."

He rarely called her Sharlee. She wasn't sure if she liked it. On his lips, it sounded proprietary. Personal. Intimate. She spent many nights dreaming of what it would be like to be claimed by him. A non-fraternization rule would have helped her resolve to keep her hands off her boss, but not at night or in her daydreams. Damn. She was definitely in trouble. Mixing love and business was never a good idea.

She opened her mouth again, but he put his hand up to halt her words. "We not only liked your work, but we also liked you. A lot. You showed you could work independently but could learn to be a team player when required. These last months have shown that you're the perfect fit for us. You're part of our family now. So like it or not, Monroe will attest to the fact that you are now a woman with too many protectors. Until tonight. Then you have just enough."

Her nose had that distinctive tingle of the formation of tears. She rubbed it. Her sigh got a little watery. "I guess I had no idea. I mean, I knew we got along fine, and there are plenty of hints about you all being Neanderthal men, but I guess I don't know what to say exactly."

She loved it, but she couldn't let on. Even after she lost her dad, she'd always felt safe, but it wasn't the same as knowing who was looking out for you. Now she did know who was looking out for her. They protected her and contributed to her sense of security. And her part was to stay as safe as she could.

But she wasn't ready to tell them that. Not yet.

"So you now understand why I'm going to roast your butt." He rubbed his hands on his thighs.

"What? No, I'm not okay with that. Besides, it doesn't explain why at all."

Her heart was racing, and her stomach's churning began again, only for a different reason. She'd never told anyone how much she dreamed of living a dom/sub bedroom lifestyle. Well, she thought she'd like it. No one had ever spanked her as a child, but that was very different from an adult engaging in spanking. She had no actual experience other than the very short boyfriend and that one swipe from Jac.

She tried to control her responses to the idea of Jac's large hand covering her butt by reminding herself this wasn't about sex, or bedroom games, but her job. Her pink bits were slick as she wiggled, and she was sure her panties were wet. She didn't dare move again for fear of leaving a wet spot. Monroe pulled out a rubber paddle from somewhere and Charlotte wasn't going to ask from where.

"You can't do that you know," she said when she finally spoke again over her tight chest and pounding heart.

"I can if you let me."

"But why?"

"We care about you, and you just made a colossal error in judgement that could have cost you your life. We can't have that happen again."

"It won't," she spoke with authority.

"Not after I spank you, it won't." Jac was equally confident.

"If I let you do this, it means I'm agreeing to it forever. I don't know if I can do that, and I like my job."

"Sweetheart, you'll never lose your job. You're too good, we need you too badly, and like I said before, you are part of the family now. I don't think you will ever be allowed to leave. I'm not sure I can do without you, now that I know what having you is like. Call it the best kind of job security." She hoped he meant more than her IT skills.

"If you don't allow this lesson, I will understand, but it means we'll have to do other things that help you remember to take care of yourself and to call us."

"Like what, exactly?"

"Like five a.m. PT."

"PT?"

"Calisthenics, running, you know, physical training, helps you remember not to repeat your mistakes by putting them into cadences."

"What?" Her voice was squeaky and too high. They all knew she didn't exercise more than the minimum. Just what the job mandated, and this was a job that mandated a high level of fitness, even for her. "I'm not getting up at five in the morning when I often don't finish working before three in the morning and I dare you to try to make me." She was feeling slightly more in control than a moment ago, but it didn't last.

Monroe laughed. "I wouldn't challenge Jac, honey. He is likely to take you up on it."

Jac continued. "Then you need to have a spanking. It's quick and done." She rubbed her thighs together but didn't answer. Things were getting slippery in more than one way. "You don't have to do this, Charlotte, but it will clear your conscience."

"My conscience is fine."

"Yep, because you take for granted that six co-workers stopped what they were doing to help you out, right? They were glad to do it, but it should not have happened. If you were more careful about what you did alone and where you went, it wouldn't have. If you had called us first, two would have come out, not six."

She was feeling anxious. He was right about her guilt. In addition, heaven help her. She really was curious what it would feel like. It would be her opportunity to see if reality matched her dreams. Her panties were downright wet, and her clit was twitching and the humming vibrations on uneven roads were making everything worse. Just this once. Should she satisfy her body and mind that she really wasn't into this type of thing?

When Jac spoke next, his voice was kind and gentle but firm. "You have to agree, but I hope you do because you need this." He held out his hand and, for whatever reason, she put her small hand in his and waited. Did she need this spanking because it was just who she was? She jerked her hand back at the fear her thought brought with it.

"Charlotte." He communicated patience, affection, authority in that one word, and she melted.

"Okay."

"Okay." He wiggled his extended fingers.

She, once again, put her small hand in his larger one and this time, allowed him to guide her over his lap. Suddenly, her tummy was pinging like a pinball machine. He didn't reach for the rubber paddle, and she was glad for that, however, he did pull her yoga pants down.

"Wait. Don't, you can't do that." Her breathing had become more labored. Her face was burning.

Jac chuckled. "Don't worry. I'm leaving your lacey undies." His voice darkened. "This time."

She wasn't as worried about her nakedness as she was afraid he'd find out her secret. Those darn drenched panties. The cool air soon registered on her nether lips through the damp gusset, causing her to clench her bottom. Regardless of her preparation, the ferocity of the first swat startled her. He had allowed her to keep her flimsy covering, whether it was for her modesty or another reason, and she was grateful. She'd read plenty of romances that explained the process of a spanking, but the actual punishment lacked adequate description.

When his palm landed, it created an explosion on her ass that she could not breathe through or space out from, even if she'd tried. The second one she thought she was prepared for, but she rocked away to avoid the strike. He hit center mass anyway. That hurt.

A lot.

"Stay still, young lady, unless you need the rubber paddle?"

She shook her head. Number three drew a squeal, and she clenched her bottom muscles even tighter. Tears filled her eyes. She squeezed them to stop the overflow. The fourth swat slammed into her throbbing buttock the moment she relaxed them, and she began to beg.

"Oh my lord, Jac, you have concrete hands. Please be done." She could feel her arousal, regardless of the heat she knew was radiating from her backside.

"One more," was all he said, and then he laid it down.

It was a scorcher. Her whole ass moved, and she cried out with the last one. Just five sensationally stinging swats and it was over. His hand was paddle enough. She'd never survive any more. Tears stung her eyes but didn't fall. The heat of embarrassment rose up her neck and diffused into her face. It was further humiliating when she remembered Monroe was also in the vehicle, but he never said another word.

Later, she figured he was a witness to the event in case anything came of it in case she accused Jac of anything. She wouldn't put it past them to have recorded everything. It hurt her to think they'd feel the need for that precaution.

After the swats were over, Jac waited as though he knew she needed a moment to herself, and she was mortified that her panties and pussy were so slippery it was physically uncomfortable. She wanted to remove the wisp of material. This was more than she had bargained for. At least it verified her love of spanking.

She was still aroused, embarrassingly excited, and she hoped she was the only one who knew but she thought she could smell her own arousal making her wonder what his scent mixed with hers would smell like, their own special lover's blend. She almost giggled. Jac never gave any indication that he discovered her secret. Jac replaced her pants and then pulled her up onto the seat next to him. He put his arm around her, pulling her into his chest. He allowed her to sit up when they arrived back at the office.

"Jac, no one hears that recording, you got me? No one."

He looked stunned for a minute, as though he couldn't believe she had figured that out. Then nodded seriously and said, "Got it." And that was all that was said about any of the actions in the car.

Once they were in the office and everyone had returned, Sharlee chastised the men she had just grown to love that much more. "You know guys I have to learn to live alone. I need to be able to handle things myself again. Cut the apron strings."

"Not happening, Sharlee, and you do live alone. We just make sure you're safe. It isn't as if we're in every aspect of your life," said Garrett.

"Right," she said with the proper eye roll accompaniment. "I need to do stuff alone because I'm an adult and that is what adults do." She lowered her voice and turned to Jac who was off to the side of the group. Though she spoke in hushed tones, the others still heard her say, "And I don't want you smacking my butt anymore."

"Why?"

"Because it's just not done."

"Yes, Shar, but you're ours and until you get your own protector, this is how it's going to play out." Monroe seemed to think there was no question.

"Stop calling me that. And what makes you think you can spank me if you don't like the outcome?"

"What makes you think we can't?" asked the ever-pragmatic Mark.

"Okay, so not *can't*, but how about *shouldn't*?" said Charlotte.

Kaden was obviously amused by the whole conversation. "Really?"

"Nah, we spank our women and like I said, until you get your own primary protector, we're it," Garrett said.

"And if you think we go away when you get an appropriate guy, you're wrong. We just join forces and back down when he needs to take over," Monroe added.

Carter, not to be left out, added, "When someone we care about needs something, we do what we can to meet that need. Sometimes, our women will need a little backside addressing and we will do that."

As she walked away, she overheard Mark or maybe she was meant to hear him. "She must have gotten off light because five swats per cheek are Jac's standard for his girlfriends, and not a one thinks to mouth back for at least an hour."

Sharlee understood she was a new experience because there never had been a woman on the team, but Mark's claim, overheard several times since she had signed on, that Jac believed in ten for stupid, twenty for naughty was more than she would ever be able to take. She shuddered even to consider it.

She moaned. They were protective, possessive, and fierce, and God help her because she believed every word they said. It wasn't just creating and building this job she was going to spend long months working on, it would also be spent building a privacy fence around her life. She mentally smiled. Maybe she could put in one or two little windows for rescuers.

Chapter 3

J ac stared at the report Charlotte had sent him. The little minx had distracted him again. Yes, it was her job to give him the report, but he wondered if she waited until he was tired so his defenses against her would be down.

The time seemed to have flown since Charlotte's tow truck incident. She had been careful to follow orders since her first encounter with his way of handling violators of the female team variety. Hell, who was he kidding? It was the way he dealt with his women, and he wanted her for his own.

His thinking head knew it wasn't feasible. She was his employee. His smaller but more insistent head didn't. He wasn't sure how long he could resist her. He'd lasted a year and some days the need was so strong; it was painful to see her. If their days ran counter to each other, it was painful not to see her. He was a mess and Jacquard Reynaud was always in control, until Charlotte.

She was one of the best things he could have ever done for the business and the team. It seemed that every time Jac turned around, someone was saying how glad they were that Sharlee was onboard. Clients rarely met her, but her results were remarkable. She'd been a real find, that was for sure. He hoped she'd quit taking even the smallest jobs for other entities soon. In the beginning, her contacts that were often different from

46

the other teammates' was helpful. It was becoming fewer and further between that her connections helped their work, and he was just biding his time before he suggested she stop taking them.

The guys trickled in for the meeting and soon the only one they didn't have at the table was Charlotte. Jac opened his mouth to send Mark after her but sounds of retching stopped him. Every mother's son in the conference room ran to Charlotte's office two doors down. Garrett got to her first, grabbing tissues, while Monroe yanked the headphone off her head, disconnecting it from the computer. Jac watched the scene unfold on the screen and understood why his Charlotte was tossing her cookies. The violence was graphic, and the audio was even more gruesome.

"Shut it down," Jac said.

"No!" Charlotte yelled. "Just mute it," she growled. "You need to see it." She gagged again.

"What the hell, sweetheart?"

Jac had replaced Monroe and moved the two of them from her office to the breakroom while everyone else viewed the screen, her office door shut. He handed her a bottle of water and shuffled her down one more door to his office, pulling her into his lap.

When she seemed to have gained control again, he asked a question. "I know what it is, but where did you find it?"

She stood in her agitation, and he didn't stop her but kept a hand on her thigh. "In your client's email. I got their log in and permission, so without pulling it off the server, I can get a copy of what they get. It was nothing useful until this video. I haven't traced where it came from and I haven't had a chance to identify anyone on it, but it was sent to them just a few moments ago. They aren't home, but they can access it anytime, anywhere. I'd call them and tell them not to open it until we get a chance to analyze it."

Garrett was in the doorway and his face was grim. "Our client is on that video."

"What?" Charlotte sat down heavily in a nearby chair. Jac pulled her back into his lap. "Is he dead?"

Garrett shook his head. "He wasn't one of the victims."

"Oh God." She raced to Jac's bathroom and started gagging again. She put up her hand in refusal when anyone tried to help her. Finally, she emerged, retrieved a toothbrush from the break room, and returned to clean her mouth.

Jac said nothing for a few moments as the rest of the guys crowded inside his office. Turning to Charlotte once she exited from the bathroom, Jac said, "You do not look at that video again and that's an order. Do you hear me, Charlotte? A direct order." He meant for her to understand how serious he was. "I'll get one of the guys to run it through the recognition program to identify the other people on it."

"No, just give me a few moments. This is my job. It just surprised me and then to actually know one of the psychos of the world, well, it's difficult. I don't have to listen to the, um, audio and can put it in a frame-by-frame format. That will help me separate from the realities of it. I was just so shocked that I couldn't process it quickly enough, that's all. But Jac, if our client is a monster, then who are we to save him from vigilantes seeking justice?"

Jac didn't answer her, instead he shooed them out of his office so he could call Mr. Hanson, their client. Before he closed the door and placed the call, he took Charlotte's face into his hands, he connected with her, purposely invading her senses. "Listen to me. I get that it is normally your job." He put his forehead to hers. "But you are more important than getting the men identified and if we need to give it to one of the other guys, even other agencies and call this job quits, then we do. Understood?"

"Yes."

"Now, honestly, do you want me to give this to someone else?"

"I want to try, Jac. Let me see if I can do it. I promise to tell you if I can't."

"Don't make me have to pull out the paddle."

She laughed. "Only you would find a way to bring spanking into the conversation."

He grinned and kissed her lips quickly. She stopped smiling; her eyes dilated in arousal, a look of surprised longing that he wanted to do something about.

"Jac—"

"Hey, do you want... oh, sorry." They separated stiffly. The moment was broken and Jac wanted to believe it was for the best, but he was sure their time to explore the attraction would be soon, very soon.

Sharlee gave Carter an embarrassed smile as she left Jac's office to work on the video. Jac waved Carter into one of the chairs he had in front of his desk while he picked up the phone to apprise Hanson of the intercepted email without sharing all they knew. Hanson was unavailable.

"Jac, you know if you are as attracted to Sharlee as she is to you, you should feel free to act on it. We are all good with it."

Jac cracked a small smile. "Good to know."

Carter returned a sheepish grin. "Well, you know. In case that was a concern."

The guys reassembled in the conference room after Kaden and Sharlee had worked on the video. Seems the others were on the same page as their teammate. "Sharlee is right, Jac. If we're supposed to vet Hanson's overseas visitors, which are soon to arrive, are we protecting him from what he should be paying for? Keeping his enemies away?"

The conversation went back and forth until Jac spoke again. "All this debate is good exercise but seeing justice for crimes isn't our call on this one. The state's attorney general asked us to do this job. We don't make judgements. We do what we are being paid to do and no more. When we are done, we get out."

Charlotte spoke in a deadpan monotone as she appeared at the conference room door. "You might not be able to do anything or choose not to do more, but I can. Darryl Hanson's name is really Baako Mador Nnamani. Evidently, the U.S. is staying out of it, on the surface anyway. He is wanted for human atrocities in several places in Africa. It isn't known that it's his name, nor is his list of crimes being advertised but it's him. There is no doubt. I'm trying to find identities on the others but so far, nothing."

"Okay, so what's the plan, Jac? Do we bail on this one?" Monroe was always first to prod the team to a solid strategy.

"Nope, we were hired to vet the guests. We can do our job, gather our pay, and then drop the rest in the State Department's lap and walk away."

"What it tells us is that one or more of his guests is watching him and will probably be on the invitation list. But the client won't want him in attendance." Garrett was drawing some sort of geometric design on paper. It helped him think.

Mark's calm steady voice spoke next. "It's a set up. I'll lay odds Nnamani or the State Department want them here, all of them, so they can handle things on their terms. You know, capture, and turn over for some goodwill with an African government they need a little human capital with."

Kaden said, "Like benevolence credit."

"Exactly what it sounds like," grumbled Garrett as he continued to draw.

"Our first order of business hasn't changed at all. It's to vet the guest list and add additional security as requested. The final list is coming today," Jac reminded everyone.

"I have it," said Charlotte.

"Sharlee, want me to work it with you?" offered Monroe. "Please? Come on. Carter is on a job this afternoon, but I think I can be a good helper."

Monroe put his hand in the small of her back causing an irrational but definite jealous response to hit Jac right between the eyes. Logically, Jac knew all the guys on the primary team were fiercely protective of their female member, but Jac's feelings went past that, way past that. Much as he wanted that woman, his libido had never and would never interfere with covering down when needed. And if he wasn't the one protecting her, there were no other men he would choose to take that task on than these men. He swallowed the response.

Jac watched Charlotte try to bring things back in line after her initial surprise, but knew it was with great effort. She was tough but had a tender heart and knowing men tortured others just because they wanted more power or to exhibit the power they had, disgusted, and hurt all of them but it affected her the most.

That meant he was more in tune to the realities of those atrocities and it sucked. He was better when he could turn that part of him off. Black and white messages were easier to decode. This feelings shit made everything a potential FUBAR situation.

The next week was full of monitoring the flights, itineraries, and agendas of many high-ranking people as they arrived for Hanson's family event. Two nights before the wedding, the screened and vetted list with the people and their known associates were sent to Hanson, aka Nnamani, and the Attorney General. It was up to their two groups of resources to protect the family and wedding party on the wedding day and beyond.

Jac's group was to monitor the house for strange goings on until the day of the wedding. At midnight of the day of the wedding, Jac's team was off duty. Two nights and one day and their involvement would be concluded. A day they were all looking forward to. He hated that Charlotte had been traumatized by the video, but after some time to take a breath, she worked the list with determination to finish the job and drop Hanson. Jac couldn't have been more proud of the way she got the job done.

"I'm monitoring from home tonight, Jac."

"You need company?"

Charlotte hesitated. "Nah, I'm good. Since we've turned over the list, nothing else should happen. I'm sure we aren't the only ones who are watching, even if unofficially. I have no doubt that Hanson slash Nnamani guy has his own watch-dogs."

"Okay, just have us dialed the minute you see anything. However, I highly doubt there will be anything tonight."

"Don't worry, I will call if necessary."

Chapter 4

The closed-circuit feed helped to see if they needed to tweak things in the electronic security, and they had. Now, there were no holes in the coverage, so she could monitor from home instead of having an additional on-site person. Sharlee had been working on a face recognition project for a private client while monitoring surveillance video streams with nothing worth reporting until she saw something she couldn't quite identify.

Leaving the one program to work on its own, Sharlee focused on the surveillance cameras. The shadow turned to movement, and the movement turned to a person with what appeared to be a semi-automatic weapon, and a buddy. They crouched behind the security equipment as though they were waiting for something. She was glad for her gun classes now.

Sharlee leaped from her chair and rushed into the next room to find her coat and shoes. She hit the automated alarm and called Jac before putting her shoes on. The call was answered before the first ring finished. She marveled at the way he could go from asleep to awake in under ten seconds.

"You good, sweetheart?"

"Yes, sir. But something is going on at the Hanson place. Two or more intruders. Watching. Look to have semi-automatics and waiting for something."

She could tell Jac was already on the run. "Initiate the roster." She had to grin mentally. What Jac called initiate the roster, she did with one push of a button. "Then connect us as each check in."

"I'll do it on my way."

"Negative. You stand down. Watch the com. Charlotte, I mean it."

"Jac, I can do that from anywhere. I'm wired for sound."

"Stand down. Do you hear me? This could be dangerous."

Charlotte snorted instead of acknowledging his edict. Jac was a tough guy when on a job and she was sure she'd have some penance to pay when it was all over with. But really, what could the man do?

She shivered when she thought of what he probably would do.

"Gotta go. Garrett is answering his call."

Better to tell truths then lies. If this bit her on the butt, at least she'd have the fact that she didn't lie. It was big. She answered her other line.

"Garrett here, talk."

It took less than a minute to relay the information. She had already sent the coordinates and information to everyone on their phones. Sharlee grabbed her favorite pistol and her black jacket. She was going to do her damnedest to stay out of things but if she needed to, she'd be prepared to help. Sharlee loved the techie side. She didn't want to do this "under cover of darkness" as her job, but she was the closest to the scene. She estimated she'd make it there right after Monroe because he always drove like a bat out of hell. Garrett and Jac were the farthest. Carter and Kaden just north of her. Mark was on Garrett's way.

Driving the five miles, she was glad in that moment that she had her gun license and knew how to use her pistols. She was comfortable with them. Charlotte had endured months of teasing that turned demanding after the infamous tow truck incident. Evidently, it became imperative that her lack of self-protection was addressed.

The guys had sent her to a three-day gun familiarization class. She had gone back on her own to train and target practice for the next few months. After the initial gun class, she was enrolled in the team's mandatory two-week self-defense class. Afterwards, she'd taken a two-month class with a local gym and did monthly reviews. She could teach the class. Now, six months after the tow truck incident, she was an accurate shot and could kick ass. She grinned. The guys didn't know it yet, but she could take care of herself.

She stopped a block away. Monroe had done the same coming from the opposite direction. Sharlee kept watching the com and saw when Jac checked in for updates.

"Status."

"Monroe on scene. Garrett has Mark six miles out from your location. Carter and Kaden two miles out. Targets have been joined by a third but are still waiting on something. No recognition is possible. Where are the cops? I'm connecting the guys into the com."

The men talked strategy. Monroe came back on. "Where the hell are the cops? I've got three from my location in the back corner. Holding position. A dark SUV has pulled up. Not ours. It's too dark to tell for sure who's inside and my goggles can't see clearly that far. Probably a neighbor, but it is too early and too late for visitors. I'm hoping for civilian and yet not. I'll have one of the guys stop and check it out. No one has exited but if I go to check, I'll expose myself."

Damn. He'd made her, and she didn't think about the fact that she had traded her other car in that week because of the extra equipment she'd needed to store and use. Now she'd have to tell them she was the unknown. Just as she opened her mouth to do that, there was movement in the yard.

She reported the change. "The other team members have arrived, and our targets are moving toward the house."

"I'm on scene," added Jac.

Charlotte wasn't cut out for this kind of firsthand drama. She was considerably more anxious than she had expected. What the hell made her think she should show up? Mainly because she was tired of her teammates treating her as if she were spun glass until she violated something in their macho code. Then her butt was handled without any finesse at all. Well, really only Jac did that, and it had been a couple of times. But it still galled her that she wasn't seen as a full member. They talked a good talk but when it mattered, she was pushed to the back of the operation.

Monroe did the "Alpha Charlie" most often. Garrett explained that was "ass chewing" and Monroe did it incredibly well. He must have gone to "Alpha Charlie" school. She'd thrown her gym shoe at him once when he demanded she go home and get some sleep.

Yeah, that went over like a lead balloon.

Sharlee ran the silent alarm again as she flipped on the inside cameras. She wasn't supposed to have a screen inside, but she didn't care. She never let everything go until they were done with the job. This one wasn't quite done. Oddly, she couldn't find anyone home. The window that showed someone standing and watching must have been a room that didn't have a camera. It must have been one of the empty guest rooms.

She looked at the screen. "Guys, something isn't right. There's movement in the front corner as well. I can't tell for sure, but the house seems all quiet except there's someone in the far back upstairs window. I don't have access to that corner of the house."

Kaden spoke up. "You have inside surveillance?"

"Um, yeah. Jac, I..."

Carter asked. "Authorized?"

"Save it for later. Give me a sitrep for the grounds."

"One man in the tree in the back yard," she said.

"Moving in that direction," Mark said. "Talk to me, Sharlee."

"Regardless of the occupant in the window, no one is answering in the house," Charlotte informed the guys.

Could they be that sound of sleepers? Or are they all gone? Then who was the mystery person in the window? They were supposed to be home. Why were the rooms she could see silent?

"Jac, the window is empty now. I wonder if he was watching for the arrival of those on the ground."

"Or us," finished Kaden.

Jac's voice was quiet but clear. "Pull the whole alarm, Sharlee. Let's hear the scream." The guys continued to say cryptic words and grunts Sharlee didn't follow. "Everyone on the ground," instructed Jac. "Find your target."

"Alarm pulled. Nothing. What's going on? I'm manually calling it in." She looked away from the streaming as she made the call.

The com went quiet. She waited. She watched her screen and the yard. It was a huge area with fencing. There were body movements but very little sound. Where was Hanson's security detail? Charlotte held her tongue. Her guys were silent doing what they had been trained to do. She didn't have that type of training and she didn't want it.

"Two targets are now sleeping," said Mark.

"I have another down," added Monroe.

"And number four is resting quietly," verified Kaden.

"On their... Jac!"

There was a blur of movement on the screen. She pulled out her Glock 22. She watched Jac out of the corner of her eye come around the side very carefully. Unfortunately, he wasn't the only one with night vision. He was joined by a second intruder. Sharlee screeched. She didn't mean to, but it just flew out of her mouth as Jac took care of his attackers with help from Carter.

Within seconds her door jerked open. She automatically pulled her weapon, getting into position without thought. It was Garrett.

"Down!" He growled, simultaneously knocking her gun out of his face and onto the seat.

She did as he said, falling into his chest between his left shoulder and the steering wheel. He shoved her further down as he fired over her left shoulder as her heart pounded out of her chest. Her breath held tight in her lungs. The front passenger window in her brand-new car exploded, and she temporarily lost her hearing. She screamed as she was jerked out of the car, her pistol landing on the floorboard.

Garrett hugged her. "Hell darlin'. You good?"

She could hear him faintly and nodded. Tears welled up in her eyes. Garrett pulled her even closer. Before too long, a less bulky but no less solid man replaced Garrett's body. The feel and the unique male scent told her it was Jac. His body told of suppressed anger. The hand at the back of her neck, sliding up to grasp her hair told her it was his possessive hold. The menacing tone in her ear told her she was in deep kimchi.

"Sweetheart, you have so much to explain to me that I'm not even going to begin it here." She shivered, and he kissed her ear. She could hear his labored breath. "I want you to get in the car with Garrett. Go to the office." They heard sirens in the distance.

Suddenly she was so very tired. "But I didn't sleep yet. And my car!" She hated the whine that accompanied her words.

He patted her bottom gently and pushed her towards the car. "Go with Garrett and sleep on my couch in the office. No arguing unless you want to discuss why you were here when this shit hit the fan. I guarantee you will be spending the next few hours answering questions with no possibility in sight. We have to clean this up. You were never here, understood?"

"Okay, okay, but Jac, there was no one in the house that I could see on surveillance but there was someone. He or she was watching everything. I'm sure of it. I didn't look everywhere but..." She shrugged. "Oh, I need my gun."

"Your... Get it," he rumbled, "and you have one minute to get your sassy, disobedient ass out of here."

He looked at Garrett then Kaden who had joined them. They seemed to have some kind of nonverbal three-way communication in a look. She'd never win around these men, but try as she might, she couldn't imagine life without them. And no matter how irritated Jac got with her or vice versa; she couldn't walk away. She was definitely in trouble in so many ways. When Sharlee stepped away from her vehicle, Kaden stepped in. Hopefully to monitor her equipment. She left with Garrett who silently drove her back to the office.

Just as they were approaching the building, she asked. "Are you okay?"

Garrett turned quickly to look at her before putting his eyes back on the road and his hand on hers. "Of course, you?"

"Yes. I'm sorry."

"I know, but I won't say you didn't scare me shitless, and you did disobey orders. But I'll let Jac handle the Alpha Charlie on this little adventure."

"I can imagine he'll handle it in more than one way."

Garrett pulled into the parking spot in the garage. "Probably. You prepared for that?"

"I think so. I'd probably do anything Jac told me to. Makes me a pathetic person, right?"

"Nah, makes you Jac's best discovery. And hon, if you did what Jac told you, we wouldn't be in this car together right now."

Her sigh was her response. Garrett patted her leg and exited the SUV.

Coming around to help her from the vehicle, he reached in and opened the glove box. As she jumped down from her seat to head for the elevator, Garrett's arm wrapped around her waist. He leaned her over his arm. Next came a streak of pain racing across her butt and it forced out a yelp. Quick as that it was done.

"What the hell?" she asked as she looked back to see the rubber paddle these men kept in the glove box. They said it was for their dates. She wondered.

"I needed to have one good swat to reinforce that you scared me shitless out there and to remind you that you can never put yourself in that kind of danger again. You got me?"

She reached back and rubbed her stinging bottom. Her lower lip came out in a pout. "Yes. Do you feel better now, you gorilla?"

"Yes thank you, much better." He tossed the paddle back in the glovebox and reached to gather her into his arms. "We like you too much to let anything happen to you on our watch. Come on darlin', you should get what sleep you can now."

Sharlee lay down on the couch. She was so tired but couldn't seem to sleep as she restlessly moved on Jac's sofa.

Chapter 5

"Charlotte, wake up sweetheart." Sharlee smiled. She was having a nice dream. "Charlotte Hope, wake up."

"It's too early, Jac." She made a disgruntled face.

"Charlotte Hope, wake up, baby. I know you're tired, but the guys are going to start arriving soon. We have some unfinished business."

Her eyes opened to see the voice's owner standing over her. She hurried to a sitting position and grimaced when she noticed her slightly achy bottom. Just one swipe with the paddle did that? She didn't want any more with that evil beast. She rubbed her eyes and straightened her clothes and yawned. Jac had returned to the office, his face grim. She'd done what she'd wanted and broken the rules. Now she'd have to pay the price regardless of her reasons. That was the way Jac played the game of security.

"Charlotte, are you okay sweetheart?"

He squatted down in front of her, so they were eye to eye. His hand reached up and brushed her unruly hair from her face, tracing his thumb over her lips and she tried to suck it in her mouth. He let her for a few seconds before pulling it out and kissing her lips.

"Hmm?"

"Yes, just tired. What time is it?" Another yawn.

"Six."

"At night?"

He did smile at that. "No baby, in the morning."

"Oh."

He looked at her for a moment, searching her face before nodding as though he believed her. He stood up, so she had to crane her neck to see him. "You disobeyed me, Charlotte."

She looked down. She started talking as she rubbed her eyes again. "But Jac, I was closest. I could easily monitor from the scene because I'm tricking out my SUV. And I'm trained. And I'm not a child." She tried to look irritated but what she saw was the back of him as he walked farther away. Her expression fell into oblivion.

Jac sat in his desk chair. "No, you aren't a child, so it makes what you did worse. And where the hell did you get that gun?" He pointed toward her pack on the floor in front of her. "Do you even have a license or know how to use that weapon? And I don't mean that little course we made you go through."

She sat straighter in her indignance. "I was there to help. I bought the gun about three months ago and of course I have a license. It's for a concealed weapon and I can shoot pretty damn well. I told you before that I can take care of myself. All of you have too much testosterone to handle a capable woman. We aren't all needy." Sometime in her diatribe she'd stood up and unconsciously moved toward his desk.

"So, is this what you want?" His voice grew louder, no longer calmly replying but not quite yelling. "Do you want us to train you to go into the field and take down the targets? To do surveillance that takes days in a tree or cramped space only to take one deadly shot? Do you want to put your life on the line for stupid fucks because you crave the thrill?" He stood and roamed the confines of his large office like a caged tiger, refusing to look at her.

Her voice calmed down as she turned to watch him in his restlessness. "No."

"Great, well you can't. I won't allow you to. You are important to us. Wait. Did you say no?"

"Right, I said no. I don't like it and I wondered why I was there once things got scary. No Jac, I don't want to be in the field like that. I'm perfectly happy staying where I am, doing what I do behind a safely locked, and if need be barricaded, door. But I would never have known that if I didn't go."

Jac returned to his desk and reached next to the right-hand drawer. He pressed the privacy button and the glass surrounding his office smoked. It was soundproof and bulletproof as well. It was just one of their preventative measures. Charlotte shivered. She'd slept for several hours before Jac woke her but suddenly she knew it wasn't enough. She was already tearing up.

"Well, now you know and in a way, I'm glad that is over, but you need a little lesson, sweetheart, in obeying orders. You need to learn better safety."

"I've had plenty of hours of training in all kinds of damn safety, Jac. I've spent most of this last year learning about it, so you wouldn't have any reason to treat me like I was made of spun glass. I'm a very good shot and can teach the self-defense class."

"I had no idea. Is that where you've been going instead of out with the group sometimes?" She nodded.

He continued. "Baby, I'm sorry that you thought you needed to do it to be treated as an integral part of the team, but I'm glad you did it. I'm relieved to know you can defend yourself. However, you, young lady, disobeyed my direct order. My standing order in fact and you know how I feel about that." Jac sat in his chair again and waited while she sat across from him. "Why?"

"I told you. I was closer and I guess I needed to prove I was as good as the other members of the team. That I was just as valuable."

"Damn sweetheart, don't you know you're better than any mother's son in here? You're smart and have skills none of us has. That's the purpose of a team. A good team has a group of diversely talented and skilled people that work well together to reach their common goal. You didn't do that last night, rather this morning. You could've compromised our end game. You worked against us. And where did that car come from?"

"The car is mine. I bought it earlier this week. I traded my old one in, so I could have a mobile unit tricked out. It isn't finished yet, but it'll get there. Now I have to get a new window. My insurance company will love that." She stood and stomped back towards the sofa.

"But you told no one. We're a team. We don't hide things from each other."

"Told you about what, the car? No, I was outfitting it with my gear first."

"Not allowed. We are a team, Charlotte."

"You keep saying that, but I don't feel like I'm a full part of that team. And what exactly isn't allowed, to have a life outside this office, have a gun, get my own training, to buy a new car, or to trick it out with my surveillance gear?" She bounced down on the sofa.

"Yes, well life outside this office is optional." He was serious.

"I don't want to be spanked," she said calmly before looking down into her lap.

"I get that. But I think, like me, it isn't technically true. You don't want to be disciplined, but you do want me to smack your ass. And I definitely want to do it. I want you to follow my orders and stay safe but I have dreamed of giving you another spanking."

She looked up. "I'll quit," she said, still and calm.

Jac leaned back in his chair and measured his response. "Okay, then, five in the morning, PT for a month." She stared at him in disbelief.

He shrugged. "There has to be a big consequence for disobeying my standing direct order."

Tears filled her eyes more insistently this time. She brushed them away roughly. "I hate the way I feel. I don't want punishment for my perceived crimes, but I do feel guilty to have jeopardized everyone's work and possibly their safety. It's so hard because I don't want discipline, but I do. I crave it." She stood, agitated, and threw the sofa pillow she had been clutching in Jac's direction. He caught it. "I'm so messed up, Jac. It was better when no one knew, when I didn't know, about my weird desires. I should probably move, do my work from home again."

"No one knows but me, baby, that you need this kind of life. Sharlee, you aren't messed up for having these feelings, these cravings. Plenty of people have them. Hell, it's normal around here, sweetheart. However, you're going to be sadly mistaken if you think we will let you quietly leave here. If you really want to quit, you can go. But I'll follow you. However, if you just don't want a spanking for disobedience, then do PT. But you have to choose. Now."

"Your hand will hurt."

He smiled. "You and I both know I'm about to reacquaint myself with your fourth point of contact aka your ass. And if you are too unruly, the third as well aka the upper thighs. I am spanking your ass for putting my best cyber security expert recklessly in danger and because she likes it. And so do I."

"I'm your only cyber security expert."

"You're the consummate brat, aren't you?" His expression as he talked about punishment was congenial, but now it was hard as nails and yet she felt no intimidation, no fear. How did he pull that look off? His eyes were caring, his face was granite.

"Jac, I don't want you to spank me. Garrett already smacked my ass with Monroe's rubber instrument of death when we came into the office. This is crazy," she said as her face flushed, and her heartbeat increased steadily.

She had fantasized as she had watched spanking movies since she was very young. Her dreams had been full of a man slapping her ass since she was a teen, but a rubber paddle, no thanks. That one swat hurt. It wasn't the situation she had expected to be in when it happened that first time for discipline. She did not expect it over the tow truck incident, nor did she want it this time. Jac wasn't her boyfriend or husband, he was her boss, and he certainly wasn't playing. But he would spank her. And she would let him, eventually.

"Once, Charlotte, he popped you once. I'll have a talk with him. You're mine to teach. As always, the power is in your hands, but if you make me wait too long, I'll reach for Garrett's rubber paddle as the mode of correction instead of using my hand."

"Fine. Just do it. I can handle ten swats."

"Sweetheart, you have so much more to atone for than just a stupid move. Ten won't even come close."

"No, you hurt with five. I'll never survive more than ten."

"Sweetheart, do you think I would ever do you harm? Yes, it will hurt. That's the point of a naughty spanking but I promise I will go to far. You will say red if you don't want me to continue. I'll pay close attention."

"How the hell did I get into a dynamic at work like this?"

He got up and walked around the desk. "Because you are mine and no one but me is going to put their hand on your delectable ass. Even Garrett knew to use a paddle because it would not have gone down well with his hand. That is my place."

"I don't know what to do with that information."

"We'll figure it out. Enough now. Put your hand in mine. Let's get this over with because we both have work to do."

"Standing up," she said ruefully.

"Yes, that might very well be how you work for a while today, but we're doing it now. Grab my hand."

Chapter 6

Jac was done negotiating. She wanted it. It satisfied his need to correct her naughty ass. Win-win. Besides, he'd be able to place his hand on her delectable bottom. She had scared years off his life when he found out she was on site. Exposed and calling the plays from practically inside ground zero. And when she screamed. He was sure his heart actually stuttered. He wanted to vomit the bile that filled his gut.

She had burrowed into his heart and taken up residence. He didn't know what to do about his feelings, but she'd never be able to stand in the line of fire. He could never deal well with it. Dammit, he was a professional, heart of ice when necessary, nerves of steel but this woman... she was his everything. Time he showed her how precious she was to him. Starting with her first, punishment as his woman.

He led her to the chair in front of his desk and flipped it around to face away from the desk. He had never thought about arms versus no arms on chairs. These were comfortable but not settle in for an hour, comfortable. No he had a sitting area in his office for that. The soft exhale from her sweet lips became liquid heat in his engorged cock. Suddenly, the convenience of the chair vanished. Neither of them would be sitting easily for a while today.

He had spent more hours in the gym recently and experienced more cold showers trying to tame his libido than he had as a teenager. He knew he was about at the end of his arousal rope. He wanted to kiss her submission when she slid her long, tapered fingers into his. He kissed her fingers, one at a time. She shuddered. She was as good as his if he could get a solid indication from her that she was interested. Words. He needed words, and he was ready to act on his need and hers in more than discipline. His calculations said she was ready for this, and him.

Jac released her hand against her side and slid his hands over her hips while looking into her eyes that glistened with unshed tears.

"You're okay, baby."

She sucked in a breath and nodded. "I am."

He hooked his thumbs into the elastic of the sweatpants she wore. He marveled at the fact that she didn't even wear a pair of jeans to add more protection when she went racing out of her place. She had no idea how to stay safe in the field or on site no matter how many classes she took or could teach. He intended to make very sure she understood that.

Sharlee placed her hands on his shoulders as he bent to help her step out of her sweats. She hesitated. Her eyes were pleading. She was worrying her lip in the most erotic way. He shook his head as much at her as himself. She released a soft sigh indicating her acceptance and put her hands on his chest as he lowered her pants, bringing immediate heat to every inch of his body. Did she have any idea of her effect on him?

"Good girl."

Her eyes lit up. His cock jumped. He nudged her over his lap. Her sweet submission would kill him.

Five in the same spot on each pale cheek soon turned them bright pink. She inhaled swiftly at each smack and softly exhaled as the feeling took over. It should have been enough and for the average woman he had placed in this position it had been, but Sharlee wanted this. He wanted this. He could show her even more play at another time. She would like it in play, but this was discipline.

He continued. His swats were slow, intense, and methodical, delivering a gradual, intense, and penetrating burn. She moaned and wiggled the discomfort, but she did not try to leave his lap. He had practiced this technique plenty of times, but she wasn't experienced. She may have wanted it in her mind but in reality, real discipline hurt like hell. Spanking, if it was something both participants wanted, craved, it was sensual, intimate, and incredibly hot in so many ways.

Jac was positive he'd know when she was getting the point of his punishment and when she was getting turned on. He had to pay close attention, so he could stop when it was time but not before she had gotten his message and a sampling of the sexual gratification from it. He wanted to be the one who gave it to her, brought her to completion, but not until he knew she was as attracted to him as he was to her. This would have to satisfy for now.

He'd had girlfriends, both submissive and not, kinky and vanilla. He'd enjoyed them all. One had tried to go length for length with him, showing him anything but submission. She had turned out to be a better business associate than lover though. He needed a soft and cuddly lover mixed with a fiery hot sex kitten. He needed her trust, obedience, submission: a woman that understood life with him would never be fifty-fifty. A valuable partner, yes, more important than he was in their relationship, yes, on the pedestal that he put her on, absolutely, but never equal.

His woman would be so much more to him. More than he ever was without her, and he hoped she'd feel the same. He had no doubt his perfect match was right here, lying over his knee making the cutest sounds of distress he'd ever heard. How he wanted her, needed her, had to have her. He wanted to kiss her red hot ass but stopped short of actually doing it.

He could stand back and watch, hoping for an opportunity to act on the feelings he had been harboring almost since the day he met her, but the wait was excruciating. He didn't have that kind of patience. He'd used us his store of biting his tongue instead of hers. He knew it would come to an end very soon. It had to.

He groaned at the reddening flesh of her ass as it depressed with his handprint and bounced back only to be offered up again so nicely. Soon the outline of his hand was a quickly disappearing white image that gave way to the overpowering redness beneath it. Her breathing came in hushed puffs of air. Yes, his Charlotte loved to get a spanking, and he loved giving her one. He had to remind himself that this was punishment first.

MOANING YET PRESENTING her bum for another after each swat, Charlotte wanted the purposefulness of the strikes on her bottom, but wanted the excruciating embarrassment to end. How it was that she had agreed a second time to lie across her boss's lap while he pounded out a tattoo on her ass she'd never know, but here she was. However, it wasn't long before the spanking had taken on a cadence of its own.

There was first the sting, followed by the deeper sizzle, then the tingle, and finally the hot ache. It ultimately settled into her core with a growing heat she couldn't ignore. Soon she didn't remember the awkwardness as enmeshed as she was in the sensual feel of his hand on her. And the inescapable heat. She craved this. She was molten and slippery. Her thighs became wet when she wiggled after an especially intense swat. Could he tell? Now she was back to embarrassed.

"Jac."

"You're okay baby, I'm watching."

She wondered what exactly he was watching for. Then the worry that she'd climax over his knee as he pounded into her what he thought was a lesson, became overwhelming. She wiggled to position her clit at a more advantageous angle. The message she was receiving loudest was she was more than a little attracted to her boss. If he didn't stop, she'd be giving away her closely guarded secrets.

He seemed to know instinctively when it was time to bring things to an end. Thank God. Even her thoughts were huffing breaths. The man was a master spanking machine, and she adored him. She wiggled her need. He rubbed her heated backside. Achy desperation clawed at her. She needed to come. So. Damn. Bad.

Eyes that had been squeezed shut, winked, and blinked until they could open fully to the light. She tried to calm her reactions, but her libido wasn't getting the memo. Jac now rubbed her back in slow, firm circles. As he moved back to her ass and thighs, she could feel herself nearing orgasm and that would never do.

"Charlotte honey, are you all right?"

She had to say something. But how could she? She needed a moment to get control over herself before she responded to his smoky, caring voice. "Yes." She blew out her breath. "Jac, you have to quit touching me."

She heard how urgent her tone was. Would he? Did she really want him to?

"Tell me." His tone was gentle but demanding. How did he always find a way to be comforting and authoritative at the same time?

"Jac, I can't."

Sharlee knew she had to get up before she fell under a spell that only she was weaving, maybe. Jac couldn't be experiencing the same strong attraction, could he? Was she missing the clues? Was this a blaring sign of his feeling?

He continued rubbing her back and didn't allow her to get up.

She wasn't trying hard.

"Can't or won't? What's going on in that over intelligent head of yours, Charlotte?"

She couldn't tell him, she had to plead. "Jac, I've got a lot of work to do. This is uncomfortable, and I've paid my price. Please let me up."

"Are you lying to me?"

"No. Honestly."

He knew. He had to. His hand circled slower and then lower. He touched the cleft of her wet sex. She heard his inhaled breath. He lingered. Touched her inner thighs lightly, and she knew he knew. How could he not? Complete humiliation. She did move now to gain freedom from his hypnotic hold.

"You are perfect so no matter what you are thinking, I want you to know that. But punishment is punishment, sweetheart."

There were a couple more moments of ignoring her wiggles and rubbing her back before he seemed to have come to a decision. He helped her up.

"Use my bathroom and cool your face, sweetheart. Promise me you will obey my orders and the intent of the orders from now on."

She grabbed the sweats and panties he had left on the table.

"Yes, sir, I will." She started to walk awkwardly to the bathroom, then turned to pose a question. "But why won't you let me go on site?" Was she deliberately taunting him?

Jac paused before saying, "Besides for your safety? You're a distraction I can't afford to have in the field."

He stood up and pushed her toward his private bathroom while he walked out of the office, closing the door quietly behind him. Yes, she wasn't the only one effected and now what to do with that information.

Charlotte didn't see Jac for the rest of the day, but she couldn't get his expression out of her mind when he told her she was a distraction. That could be a good thing, right? And the way he said she was perfection. It filled her up so much. She needed to break down the barrier that stood in their way. Work. Now how to do that?

Jac was turning over the Hansen job first thing this morning. Sharlee was just as eager to finish closing out the contract as the rest of the team. Everyone acted as though nothing had happened in the early hours of the morning. For that bit of mercy, Charlotte was happy. The client's daughter was more than likely married now and glad to be away from her father.

Sharlee would certainly be happy to walk away from this one. What did the guys call stuff like this, oh right a Charlie Foxtrot. That sounded so much better than a clusterfuck, well it was nicer anyway. Another reason these men wanted to call her Charlie. They sure used the word often enough. No addition to their daily vocabulary.

While Sharlee was happy for the return to routine, she knew she'd never be the same. She should have been happy that life was going back to normal, and that she distracted Jac, but things were different now. Something had shifted inside and without a doubt she knew she was falling desperately in love with Jacquard Reynaud. No, things would never be ordinary again.

After that fateful day when she had acknowledged her boss wasn't going to quit invading her daydreams and night wanderings, Jac seemed to almost avoid her. She embraced the realities of their situation, but Jac obviously had not. Since that day in his office Sharlee knew she'd either need to quit or figure something out. She decided to look for a date. Any date really, but a date was the start of getting past Jac's dark eyes and even darker hair, past her attraction for him. Or make him so jealous that he would declare he had feelings for her. She'd have to go against her nature in order to ignore him. She'd try, but it was going to be painful and necessary.

Chapter 7

Jac avoided her but watched her every move, according the Becky. "He's more distracted when you are in a meeting, wear something cute or even when you don't. He is particular to send Monroe or Garrett to give you messages, but he has his most used camera focused on your office. He stays until you go home."

"That's all find, but he needs to admit there is chemistry. If he isn't man enough or brave enough to do it, then I am going to start dating."

"Really?" asked Becky.

"Unfortunately, yes. I don't know why I chose this as the way, but it will either get him jealous or tell me he isn't going to act on his interest. At least I'll know."

Many restless days and nights of thinking and watching passed in hopes that she wouldn't have to go through with the plan. Sharlee thought she had the answer as to why Jac was avoiding intimate contact. He'd not made even the slightest hint of a move on her since that morning in his office. It must be because he saw she was attracted to him, and he wanted to stop it. Meaning he wasn't more than physically attracted. Not enough.

He had even gone to hook up with what Kaden called a "stress relief" date. The news made her angry, and the pain was torture. Then she found out he canceled at the last minute. The others had turned to look at her when she walked in on that conversation but were quick to look away when she made eye contact.

Unless work needed her in the office, she often went home early. They let her. The guys checked in with her often but so long as she was getting the job done, and she always would, things got bleaker. When Jac made a decision, he stuck to it.

"I think that won't last for long. It's already been a month, and that man is a bear with a sore tooth and a thorn in his foot. He has never been this moody. You just wait."

Sharlee did but Becky was wrong, and Sharlee must have misread all the things she thought were signs because he cut her a wide berth. So she tried and for a while she was doing well in connecting with other people, meeting them at the coffee shop and drop-in volleyball, group walks on marked trails and the like. She even went horseback riding but all she could think about was Jac liked horses.

At the end of a busy, meeting people month, she still had nothing more than one date with anyone until she ran into an old classmate outside of their offices a few weeks later. She was just at the brink of putting in her notice. Maybe that would make Jac sit up and take notice. Either he would want to keep her or not being his employee would make him more likely to jump her bones.

Kyle Martin was an old friend from Sharlee's hometown. She was surprised to find how excited she was when she saw her old high school friend. He'd been a nice guy in school, and she didn't hesitate when he suggested they go out for a friendly dinner. After the third date, he suggested they date exclusively, "to try it out."

"That's a little bit fast for me, Kyle."

She hesitated not only because of her own reservations but because of the guys in the office. She could almost hear them raise objections all over the place and she was finding herself hesitant as well. Maybe this would be her chance at spurring Jac into making a move. She would take it, but cautiously.

"Can we just agree to date but not be exclusive yet?"

"Why, got a fiancé on the side?" Kyle laughed at what he thought was a joke.

"No, no. But I think it's too soon to date in a committed way. I'm just having fun, aren't you?"

"Don't you like me?"

Charlotte almost rolled her eyes at his childish question. "Honestly? I like you as a friend and it is too early to declare more than that. It would be a lie." She knew it wasn't too early because she had been into Jac on day one and so far had not felt one spark with Kyle. "Just give us a chance to get to know each other."

Kyle had reluctantly agreed but wanted to come to her place and that gave her a chill of warning. She never brought anyone home. It left her exposed, vulnerable. If there was one thing she had learned from her cyber work and the team, it was safety first. Not understanding why it should bother her but knowing she didn't like to compromise her privacy even for a friend. Whenever possible, she avoided the subject.

At work it was even harder to keep her personal life private. "Who is that kid you were hanging out with last night?"

"Carter, were you spying on me?"

"Nope. I was picking up my dinner from the restaurant you were at."

"Why didn't you come and introduce yourself?"

"I didn't want him to think I was competition or anything. Besides, I like the hostess at that restaurant, and I spend my time chatting her up. I'm going to get a date with her yet."

Monroe picked up the thread. "And so, are you dating this guy or just going out with him?"

"Is there a difference?" Sharlee played ignorant.

Jac was there, appearing out of nowhere. If she was a vapor on the net, he was a mist on the ground. He spoke in her ear. "Are you misbehaving? You know what happens when you do."

She shook her head but shivered with that familiar thrill when Jac was intimate with her. "I'm dating him, but not exclusively."

Carter nodded. "Good. I don't mind you going out. But if you think you're getting serious, we need to know more about him first."

"Hey, I'm the one who does the deep checks on people. Besides, he says he's an online salesman for a group of small companies. An independent contractor, so we have similar interests."

Jac had already left the area, either irritated with her or satisfied with the information, she wasn't sure which. Nothing more was said, but she experienced some calculating glances and questioning looks periodically. She wasn't the only woman among these testosterone laden ex-military men, but they seemed to use their powers of protection only consistently on her. They were over juiced adrenaline-high junkies making her a prime target for their over-zealous attention.

Protectiveness went without saying and their pushing towards what they thought was best for her was the order of the day. She and Becky were their outlet except Becky handled it better than she did. The guys needed girlfriends, not just occasional dates. Until that happened, her life was full of instances where her desires and choices only played a rudimental part in how they organized her world.

Everyone except Garrett who was dating Katrina Long whom everyone called Callie. Garrett had backed off Sharlee since Callie had moved in. The woman was friendly but there was something more that Sharlee couldn't put her finger on. Maybe you had to be a little different to date one of the guys. Maybe to date her too, because she thought there was something odd about Kyle that she had never noticed before. Great, she was becoming paranoid, too.

Charlotte had her own trouble these days. The guys had even tag-teamed her once when she did go out on that first date with Kyle. That information came out later when she had caught Mark out of the corner of her eye. She read each one the riot act, and she was satisfied they understood. They didn't change.

It had been almost two months since she'd started to see Kyle and there was still no thrill. She had to admit to herself that she felt nothing and never would. She'd have to tell him tonight that she could only be his friend. It was going to be hard because he seemed interested in her.

He was always pushing to see her place and for some reason, she still had difficulty sharing her private space with him. The one thing he never tried to do was become intimate with her. Charlotte was glad because it took the pressure off her.

And yet, he was pushing for visiting her place more and more. She'd tell him at dinner tonight.

"Let's go to your place and talk about this, Charlotte."

"Nope. I'm serious when I say that I just don't like you in the way you want me to. I'm sorry but discussing it anywhere else won't change that truth."

"Well, then let's go to my house and we can open a bottle of wine and have a few laughs. You do still like spending time with me, right?"

"Kyle, I'd love to be friends but so long as you understand that is all it can be."

"Yeah, I get it."

His words were right, but his tone and the way his eyes flitted nervously unnerved her. Nonetheless, she was relieved that he had taken her words better than she'd expected so she agreed, and they went to his place. Sharlee had been there several times, usually when he'd ask unsuccessfully to coax an invitation to her place.

When they arrived at his apartment this time, things seemed off. For the first time since they had been dating, she was feeling awkward. Kyle must have noticed her reaction because he tried to be more accommodating. He seemed to flit around trying to latch onto the one thing that might relax her and him.

"Let me get some music going."

"Kyle, maybe I should just go home."

"No. I mean, hang out with me for a while. The night is young, and I enjoy talking to you."

Sharlee looked at her watch and though it wasn't late, she didn't really want to stay much longer. Kyle seemed kind of desperate for company. He entertained her, though. And he could make her laugh.

She didn't want to pity him, but she did. Nope, that was a hard line for her. Time to end this night. There was regret that they could never be more than friends, but they couldn't. Jac was always front and center in her mind. She hoped she could keep Kyle as a friend. As a lover though, the only one she could see filling that spot was Jac.

"Okay. Just an hour."

"Good. An hour is good."

He was still nervous but knowing she would stay a little seemed to take some of the pressure off him. Why he would feel under pressure she didn't know, but just an hour would be enough.

"Do you want wine? I've got the kind you like."

Uncharacteristically, Kyle tried to make a move on her, running his hand up her thigh as he shared the couch.

"Kyle, stop. Look, this was a bad idea. I need to go."

"No. Sorry, sorry. I guess I just thought that was why you didn't want to be with me because I wasn't, you know, more amorous."

"Trust me. I don't want you to be more amorous. We just don't mesh. Kyle, it's okay. It happens."

"Sure. I understand."

He got up nervously and checked the music again. He said he understood but Sharlee was getting the impression that he didn't. Then, just moments later, he rushed her and tried to kiss her while groping to make purchase with a breast. Her self-defense classes came back enough for her to punch him in the throat. She started to take him out, male specific, but stopped mid-move.

That seemed enough to stun him and ultimately, send him to the bathroom to recover.

"Don't call me ever again. No one treats me like that, and no woman deserves to have to fight off a jerk."

Sharlee grabbed her bag and rushed to the door as she tried to put her clothing back in place. She knew she would bruise but had come out much better than Kyle. As she reached for the door, there was a pounding on it. Kyle was still in the bathroom and Charlotte yanked it open.

"No, don't open it," Kyle said racing out of the bathroom. Sharlee's back slammed against something hard. She felt pinned, arms held firm, her head hit hard against the wall. She felt a wave of nausea. Others were pushing in past her.

"Hey, what's going on? Let me go! Stop leaning on me." She pushed against the officer without noticeable effect. Another wave of nausea descended.

Charlotte could feel the panic rise in her chest. The first thing she thought was to call Jac. He'd get her out of this mess, whatever the mess was. She looked over and saw another officer had Kyle pressed up against another wall before she had an inkling of what was going on.

A third officer was looking in her direction and saying something about a search warrant. "God, I don't know what you would search for, but I can't give permission. I don't live here."

The officer seemed to accept that and nodded. Her head hurt and she could hear her heart pounding in her ears, but she tried to listen over the beat, as they executed the search warrant. Sharlee listened as they described what they were looking for to Kyle who had a more than panicked look on his face.

"Why? I mean, what do you think he did?" asked Charlotte.

"What we think you both did was scam the elderly and disabled out of their money, for starters."

"What?" She screeched the reached for her head to help the pain. "You think I did what? How could you even consider that I would do something so despicable?" Too late, she noticed that her date was remaining oddly quiet. "Kyle, you didn't do that to vulnerable people, did you? You didn't take advantage of them?"

He still said nothing.

"Oh, God. Is that why you wanted to come to my place, to use me for another access point? You little..." she attempted to lunge toward Kyle but was held firm by the officer.

An enormous hand clamped over her mouth, and she fought the invasion as her eyes searched frantically for the source only to crash into a face that sent so many messages, she had to stop talking to begin reading them all.

"Miss Armstrong..." started the officer.

Chapter 8

"Is not speaking at this time," answered the human slab of granite in front of her.

Garrett meant business and all Charlotte could do was nod in agreement. Garrett was angry. Probably took him from his sexy times with Callie. She almost smiled, but she realized this wasn't funny and that Garrett was not pleased at all.

He removed his hand and raised his brow sharply when she tried to open her mouth again. Sharlee reached for her head again then her belly. She huffed in ineffectual anger and swallowed her verbal response. She was relieved she had a protector with her no matter the overbearing sense of entitlement that came with him.

They both listened to what the officers told her that Kyle had been up to because it was increasingly obvious she was not the brains of the operations. She didn't have any of the answers and asked more of her own questions to their questions.

"Garrett. I'm probably going to jail. Don't tell Jac. He might burn down the town."

"Oh, I'd count on that, my dear."

"I can't believe that jerk," she indicated Kyle with a tilt of her head. "He was stealing from all those people. And these guys think I knew about it. Please, you have to promise me you won't tell Jac. I'm going to have to move. He's going to fire me.

He'll have to. Damn, and I really loved this job, but he can't have this on the company. Besides, he won't admit he is as into me as I am into him. It was inevitable anyway. Just wait and don't tell him. Let me just disappear." The tears began to flow when her rambling stopped.

Her hands were cuffed so she couldn't even wipe them. "I won't tell him, Sharlee. I won't have to."

She sniffed. "Oh, good. Thanks." Then it sounded wrong. Something was off. "Wait, why aren't you going to tell him?" Her voice was drenched in her own tears.

"Because you already did," said Jac from the doorway. He walked up and Garrett stepped back. Jac took her into his arms and wiped her tears away. "Don't cry, sweetheart. I'll get the information we need. You don't talk to anyone but us, you got me?"

She nodded and sniffed again. "Hold on while I figure this out." He kissed her cheek and stepped back. "Garrett, stick with her. When the others arrive, they need to keep her safe. Nothing happens without me."

"You got it."

"The whole team? Crap."

Garrett grinned. "I think sitting might be optional for a while. Carter had a date."

"Shut up. I'm never dating again."

Garrett's attempt at a joke fell flat. She was going to jail. There went her clearances, her jobs, her contracts. There went her everything. She'd have to find a job that didn't require those things. God, what happened if they didn't believe her and actually charged her with something? Worse yet, what if they took her to trial? The tears started again and soon her sobs drew the attention of the others in the room.

"Dammit Garrett, I said take care of her." From somewhere a towel appeared at her face and on her cheeks, wiping them dry. Then it was at her nose. "Blow baby." She couldn't. Her nose felt completely plugged. Jac kissed her lips. Sharlee sucked in her breath. "I'll fix this honey. I won't leave you, but you're going to make yourself sick. Calm down, okay?"

She nodded and watched as Jac waved Garrett back into his protective position as Jac returned to talk to one of the officers again. She was feeling some confidence since she wasn't there alone, but it didn't stop the abject fear she felt. Sharlee watched as they walked Kyle out to the hall. As he was passing her, he stopped.

"Watch out, Sharlee. He isn't going to stop until he gets what he wants."

"Who Kyle?"

He shrugged as they pushed him past her, causing Sharlee to lose her barely restrained control. She put her foot out and made him lunge into the cop in front of him taking them both to the ground. There were some words exchanged and a small altercation in the hallway that she couldn't see. She almost felt sorry for Kyle by the time the police picked him up from the floor. Almost.

Then the whole first string appeared in the front room to take care of business, every stinking one of them. She was the recipient of hard looks, protective glances, and a human shield that they created between her and the poor cop who was trying to get her statement. Everyone occupying the same space could feel the heated male irritation that permeated the room. Testosterone: the place was lousy with it.

Sharlee looked at the officer. "I really didn't know. I came here to break it off with him tonight."

"And why was that Miss Armstrong?"

She looked over at the back of Jac who was talking to the lead cop in the kitchen area. "Because there was no chemistry."

"Well, I imagine Mr. Reynard would have noticed if his technology expert was into something like this but we have to be sure."

"Can't you let me go home while you figure things out?"

"Let me check on our information first."

"Can you at least uncuff me?"

She tried her most pitiful entreaty, then dropped her head. She knew the submissive act. She also knew that if it was Jac, he would've had something to say about her efforts at manipulation but evidently this cop did not understand that art as much as her employer.

"Hold on." The officer seemed bemused.

Within a few moments, the policeman came back and un-cuffed Charlotte. Jac spoke next to her. "Charlotte, he's a scam artist if that's what one could still call a high-tech thief these days. Evidently he was making quite a good living doing it too. They've been watching the two of you for some time as they gathered evidence."

"What? I've only been dating him for two months or so. I don't know what they were watching because except for a few times, we've spent most of our time in public. We've had the most 'G' rated relationship of all time. I haven't even," the hesitation brought her cheeks to a glowing red, "spent the night with him," she ended in a low voice. She looked up and Jac gave her a quick nod of approval. She needed that. "Look, just tell me what you need to prove I didn't have anything to do with it."

"We had a tip from a reliable source."

"Well let me tell you, whoever it was, wasn't as reliable as you think if he thought I was part of this thing with Kyle. I know for sure he had no proof of my involvement. And who was Kyle talking about when he told me to watch out? What did he mean that a mysterious 'he' wasn't stopping until he got what he wanted? Who is 'he' and what does he want? And could he be the one who turned Kyle in?"

The interviewer did not respond except to say, "This is an ongoing investigation, ma'am."

"Fine but investigate," said Sharlee.

"Charlotte Hope... stand down."

She gave Jac a mutinous look and then sighed, grimaced, and shook her head. "Fine."

The lead investigator that had walked closer with Jac said, "Good. We're going to need your personal computer and your cell phone."

"Um, okay, but that is the only phone I have, so..."

"I'll give you one of our spares, just give it to him," said Jac.

She reached in her pocket and handed it over. "I don't have my computer here. I never take it anywhere. You'll have to come with me to my place to get it."

Even though she'd been with Jac for nearly a year and a half, she evidently hadn't been working for them long enough to make the cops automatically disregard her association with

Kyle. She wondered how long it would be before she'd get a pass.

"Stay close." The officer warned.

"Yes, sir."

"Don't worry, she isn't going to be out of our sight until this thing is resolved."

She opened her mouth to respond and received the most chastising look she had been on the receiving end of in her life. Sharlee realized that Jac was in no mood for her protests, so she remained quiet as more hot tears rolled down her face. Jace reached over and wiped them away without a pause. Like taking care of Sharlee was a natural, automatic thing. Was that good or bad?

It turned out to be a very advantageous thing that Reynaud and Associates worked with the police whenever possible, which meant whenever it didn't compromise their job, the police tended to cut the team some slack. Whether because of that relationship or something else, the cop appeared to believe she didn't have anything to do with the scheme, but they needed to check further. Garrett said he'd bring the computer in that same night. The lead officer decided to send a cop with them to retrieve it.

"Take anything that will help you eliminate me. Please," said Charlotte.

Finally, she was released. Very reluctantly, she walked to the elevator caged by what would have appeared to anyone watching, that this was the Secret Service during their workout. Garrett took the keys to her car and apartment while Monroe and the cop followed them to her messy home. She was sure she'd get flack for that too. No wonder she didn't want to date anyone. Between the males in her day job and the crooks in her nightlife, she wondered if going back to "no life" would be best.

Later, after the cop had left with her computer and she had another cry, a shower, and was chewed out by Garrett.

"That isn't fair to get angry with me and blame me for something I was unaware of, so stop. I didn't know he was stealing from elderly people and those unable to protect themselves against it. At least I didn't let him come to my apartment. He'd have gotten more ideas of how to slip under the radar. I don't know why you have to focus on that mess instead of what is really scaring me."

Garrett asked, "What is really scaring you, Sharlee, because I would think this was bad enough?" His anger seemed to have been defused somewhat.

"Kyle said to be careful. That 'he isn't going to stop until he gets what he wants.' What if what *he* wants is me?"

Jac arrived to see that things were good for the evening. He seemed calm but his irritation showed through to those who knew him well enough. She was done with it all. He leaned down and gave her a quick kiss before speaking.

"Charlotte Hope, how is it that you are quite adept at finding the criminals hiding places and finding those who are criminals for work but miss the whole boat when you are dealing with your personal life decisions?"

Sharlee crossed her arms with an obvious attitude. "Don't you start, Jac, I had no idea about any of this and I won't accept any more reprimands or scolding from any of you."

She slammed into the armchair, crossing both her arms and legs. Evidently only she was impressed with her own bravado.

"Did you look up his background, Charlotte Hope Armstrong? You know, do your damn job to protect yourself?" Jacquard used her IRS name when she was in trouble. "What the hell were we supposed to do if you were arrested?"

"You used my middle name. You're obviously angry with me. Jac, I did nothing wrong. But if they had arrested me anyway, I would have expected you to call Ryker."

He looked at her with an intensity she knew wasn't sexual. He was seriously pissed. She sighed.

"I knew him from high school, okay? I didn't think I needed to check him out, sir." She always called him 'sir' when he was dressing her down. It was as though her skin was peeling off, such was the agony of having to answer a few more questions and listen to his responses.

Finally she'd had enough. She slammed her body out of the chair, stomping to the cabinet, she grabbed glasses out of the cupboard and pulled out a partially used bottle of single malt Highland whisky and held it up to the two men. She then poured her own finger of the fragrant alcohol.

"Should you be drinking?"

She ignored the question and asked, "Interested?" Both men nodded. She poured.

They savored the cherry overtones and Jac commented. "This is pretty heady stuff for my techie to be drinking."

She shrugged. "My grandfather kept me informed of the finer points of spirits. He was a sommelier. He left me with his collection of fine wines and liquors and an affinity for the finer stuff. This one is a bit strong on first taste, but I think it mellows as you sip. How about you?"

"Probably the best I've ever had," said Garrett. "I'm not really a whisky man, so that is saying something."

"I love the flavors, but this isn't my favorite. That's different for everyone," answered Charlotte. "I thought this was one of Jac's favorites."

Jac nodded and said, "Buttering me up, good call." After a few more calming moments, Jac asked about Kyle again but in a less accusatory way.

Sharlee gave him a long-suffering sigh. "For the last time. I told you I dated him because he was from my hometown. He just happened to be outside the office when I came out one day and we ran into each other."

"Didn't you think it was odd that he was so far from your hometown, in front of your building, right when you got off?"

"No. I mean, I didn't really think about it. I was there so why couldn't he be there?"

"You were there because we enticed you to be here. Did he know what you did for a living?"

"I don't think so. I never really talked about work at all. Wait, you aren't thinking that he targeted me for what I had access to or what I knew, are you?" The men were silent. "You are." She made an angry grunting noise. "I'm so stupid. I know how to get in and out without a trace. He wanted that, didn't he? He wanted Vapor, not me. But he wouldn't have known how good I am. I never told him. We didn't talk about my job or his."

Garrett spoke. "I don't know but it seems to me that if you look hard enough, and know your stuff, you can find out anything about anyone on the net."

Sharlee groaned. "That's it. How dense can one person be? He said he was trying to find a member of his family a few years back, right before I came here, and I helped him. It was easy, and I found him in a day."

"So he knew you were good." Garrett sat back. "You feel for his bait."

"I am so stupid," she moaned.

"Damn, sweetheart." That was his verbal cue to her when she had been too risky and was going over his knee. Her bottom twitched. "If you don't stop blaming yourself for this I'm going to start on that behind of yours. Your error wasn't in being with someone familiar, it was not remembering to keep your game face on and staying alert, even in the private sector. You'll learn. Your second mistake was not informing us. You've done that before, but you won't be making that mistake again."

"I don't know what I could have told you if I didn't know there was anything fishy."

"You forgot to tell us how things were progressing. Did we know he was pushing to get to your apartment?"

"Jac I'm not some child to call for help on every skinned knee. I'm not weak and I didn't know I needed help."

"And there is another mistake, thinking it is weak to ask for assistance." He tossed back the last drops of his drink and stood up. "Gotta go. You are to be in my office front and center first thing after you go to the police station and make your statement. Garrett will stay with you. He'll know if we need to bring in Ryker."

"Ryker Bennett? Your attorney? I'll pay you back. Tell him to send me his bill. I know it doesn't matter if I did anything wrong or not. He will at least not make me look guilty. Why won't you believe me?" Sharlee stood.

Jac grabbed her upper arm. "I know you are not guilty. That's why you aren't sitting in a room being grilled by Ryker right now in preparation for tomorrow. It's why you aren't in jail. Why I'm letting you to go with one escort to the cop shop. It's why you can sit right now. We believe you but it isn't us you have to convince, it's the police. So, be a good girl and follow the rules or I'll have to call in Ryker immediately and it will look like you're guilty because you have gotten representation."

"You know that isn't true, right? It's smart to bring in your attorney right away if you think it might go sideways."

"These guys know you work with us. They know we vet our people well. They also know that if you are really good and work for me, that you are likely good enough to do and hide what you do very well."

"What a mess, Jac."

"I know baby. I promise we will fix this." He drew her close for a quick hug before letting her go. "I'm going to dig into Kyle's background or rather Kaden is."

"I could do it... oh, no computer. But I have others. And there are the computers at work and my car." She gave Jac a shocked look. "My car. My equipment. Where is everything?"

"I have it secured in my garage at my home. No one will bother it." He dropped another kiss on her lips. "Go to bed. Now. You need to get to the cop shop early."

"Fine. I won't sleep but if you wanted to stay..." Jac shook his head. "You know that wouldn't be a good idea."

"Maybe not, but it would be fun."

Jac shook his head and smiled. Taking Garrett with him, they stepped outside for a chat and when they were done, only Garrett returned.

Chapter 9

The next morning things happened as expected. The questions the cops had by the time she arrived were much less invasive than Jacquard's had been. Luckily, the cops were convinced she was innocent. They'd return her computer in a few days. They gave her the cell phone immediately. Jac walked in as they were nearing the end of the interview.

"We checked your phone, Miss Armstrong. Mostly office calls. A few local calls, a call to your parents once a week, and our suspect, that's it." She didn't say they were never that efficient, so she was fairly sure they just checked her phone log, not her deleted history or anything else. Her calls to clients were from a different phone and often from an encrypted computer program.

"I told you my life was pathetic and certainly nothing that would equate to stealing. If I was going to steal, I'd more likely steal myself a life."

The officer gave her a pitying smile and let her leave with Garrett and Jac.

"Why are you here?" she asked her boss as they stepped out of the station.

"I called Garrett and got the information about you probably being dropped from the suspect list, but I wanted to be sure you didn't need anything." He looked at Garrett and said, "I had Kaden drop me off, so I could ride back with you."

Jac's phone rang, and he waved them inside the vehicle as he talked and walked a small area outside the car.

"I'm sorry," said Garrett after they climbed in the car.

"About what, exactly?"

"About the invasion of privacy."

She sighed and smiled in his direction as he started the car. "Thanks, but since it is obvious, I have nothing to hide, there isn't anything to be sorry about."

"You know Jac has a soft spot for you."

"Does he? I wish it were true. I thought so at one time but now?" She shook her head. "I'm just trouble."

"No, you aren't *just trouble*." Garrett's voice was gruff. "You bring sunshine to our work. You're bright and energetic, and we would be less cohesive if you weren't there to pull our heads out of our collective asses sometimes. Don't you ever forget what a strength you are to this team."

"Thanks."

They silently waited on Jac. After the call was finished, he said a few things to Garrett and then slid into the back seat with Charlotte. She looked at him oddly. The front seat was available, but he sat with her, raising her heart rate and her hopes. As the car pulled out on their way to the office. Jac talked.

"Listen, sweetheart. It's time to learn when to ask for reinforcements and when it's time to bail out."

"I tell you again, I didn't know that he was into anything hinky. I mean, I went to high school with him. Besides, I was ending the dating part last night."

"And that's the only precaution you took, that you went to school with him ten years ago? You need a few more swats for that. You need to clear the background checks with Garrett before you go out with another guy. Before we're done here, you will agree to that."

"I won't do it, Jac. That isn't fair. You don't clear your dates."

His voice raised slightly less than hers had. "What isn't fair is hearing your name on the damn police channel. What isn't fair is everyone coming at breakneck speed to pull your sassy ass out of the fire."

"You didn't have to come. I didn't ask anyone to help. I didn't call anyone," she said resentfully and a bit loud except she sounded like a pouty teen. "I could've handled it myself."

Jac's frustration was at the limit. "Your talking privileges have been revoked until we get to the shop."

The shop was their name for the office. Why, she could never figure out, but it was.

"Do you understand that they were going to arrest your sassy ass and figure it all out later?"

"But I didn't do anything. I'm fucking tired of telling you, I made a mistake. You know, like humans do."

"Did you hear me say they'd figure it out later? That later could've been today, tomorrow, or next week. You have a lot of explaining to do."

"Maybe I'm too much trouble and I should just quit."

Jac shook his head. "You are way too old for dramatics, young lady."

"I need to go back into hiding anyway because Kyle implied that someone not nice wouldn't stop until they got what they wanted and evidently I am part of that quotient."

"And you told no one about this?"

"I told Garrett right after he said something to me. You haven't given me any opportunity to sit down and work on the puzzle. I'm always trying to volley answers to your question and accusations. It's all your fault any of this happened, anyway."

The car went silent. Not a sound outside of driving noises and traffic.

"Charlotte, what are you talking about? How could I have made this not happen?"

"Nevermind. I'm just done with everything. Garrett, can you just take me home, please?"

"I can. Is that what you really want to do? You're going to need a bodyguard so who do you want with you?"

"Do I have to?" She was exhausted and pleading came easy in this state of mind.

"I'm afraid you do, hon." Garrett was being so unlike himself. He wasn't chewing her out or telling her what she should do or anything. It was hard to handle. And his voice was gentle. That couldn't be good.

Jac silently held out his hand. She sighed and placed hers in it. She was hauled over his hard and uncomfortable lap without another word. It didn't matter that she had yoga pants on, she might as well have been naked for all the protection they offered.

"Don't spank me hard, Jac. I didn't do any of this on purpose and I'm shattered."

He rubbed her ass and the small of her back. She simply laid there in both anticipation and rising libido. How could she be affected by him when he was being so deliberately obtuse in this matter?

"I said your speaking privileges were revoked, sweetheart." His words were what she expected, but his tone was almost loving.

He punctuated his reminder with two hard slaps to her southern cheeks before going on to teach the lesson she was evidently too slow to grasp. Five substantial slaps in the same spot, on each cheek, with no reprieve or words interjected between his slaps and her cries of discomfort. He stopped his lesson to rub her backside, and the heat melted her core into a pool of need.

She did her best to keep talking because he had said she couldn't talk. Childish? Yes. Did it give her a moment of satisfied control? Oh, yes. He added several extras to the sit spots, and she yelled her complaints to no avail. As always, she was oozing honey and her panties were drenched. This was strictly business, and her boss was making sure he did his job thoroughly. But was it? He knew what this did to her, and she whined her frustration. She was angry. Didn't really agree with this interpretation of the events. What was wrong with her? She craved his care through discipline. She was hopeless.

Five in the same spot hurt like the devil and he continued to alternate cheeks until she begged, then he rubbed her bottom as though sealing in his lesson and his tender care. Making her crave him more. As he did the first time, he sat her in the seat next to him but unlike the first time it wasn't what she wanted.

She didn't care that Jac knew she was wet due to his actions. She wanted him to coddle her. She wiggled restlessly, sniffling longer than technically necessary. He sighed and pulled her onto his lap and cushioned her head against his shoulder. She snuggled in and hissed when she put pressure on the breast that Kyle had manhandled.

"Bottom sore?"

His question wasn't teasing, but she didn't think he was unaware.

"No, my bre... um, yes, my bottom is sore. Don't gloat."

"Charlotte, you were going to say something else. What?" That's the old, demanding Jac.

"What? Nothing. I was going to say my butt hurt."

"Do you need another spanking?"

"No, God no."

"Then talk."

"Okay but you can't be angry."

His sigh was resigned. "What hurts Charlotte?"

She hesitated when a smack hit her exposed left hip. "Okay, okay, it's my breast. There wasn't any pressure on it during the, um, in the other position but it does hurt. Last night, when I said I just wanted to be friends with Kyle, he... he tried to, you know, touch me."

He was immediately alert, and she sensed Garrett sit up stiffer. "Did he do anything against your will? Assault you?"

"No Jac, nothing other than manhandle me some."

His voice gentled. "Let me see, sweetheart."

"What? No! I'm not exposing my boob for you to ogle."

"Let me see it or I will take you to the emergency room and we will file an assault charge."

"Fine!" Charlotte yanked up her tee shirt and gingerly pulled down the cup showing the afflicted breast. She hadn't seen it yet, but she allowed him to look his fill before checking herself. His lip tightened to a thin line.

"Damn, baby. That's going to look ugly. Garrett did you see this?"

"No, dammit, and he isn't going to see it. God Jac, sometimes I wonder about you," she declared as she carefully returned her clothing to its correct position.

"Are you sure you don't need to file a report?" asked Garrett from the front. There was no laughter in his voice, only seriousness.

"I think you should, baby."

"I'm not showing my breast to anyone else. I shouldn't have shown you."

"Yes, you should have. You shouldn't have tried to keep it a secret."

"Can we just forget it? It's just another painful reminder of the disaster my life is." Was she always begging? Her life was so much less complicated when she worked from her apartment anonymously. But lonely.

"We can stop talking about it," said Jac.

"Good." Sharlee snuggled back into his waiting arms. She savored the closeness for as long as she could.

Garrett didn't take her home. Figures.

Charlotte worked with her desk heightened and slept on her tummy that night. She dreamed of a tough ex-military guy who was hard as nails on the outside and soft as spun cotton on the inside. She needed nothing else to produce her orgasm the next morning but reminders of her dreams.

Charlotte slipped her fingers down her soft belly and thought of Jac. She imagined his hands had just warmed her bottom, and he was now slipping his fingers into her pink heat. He traced her labia and breached their security to the moistness beyond. His fingers were tantalizing her inner sanctum as the other hand massaged her swollen breast. Her breath came quicker as fingers strummed her needy nub.

Finally flicking her clit, she jumped at the tingling that spread the almost aching sensations throughout her center. Pulling on her nipple, she brought it to just the other side of pain as her clit stiffened under the attention it was receiving. She spread her legs wide as the sensations grew stronger. She shifted to the other breast as she imagined Jac loving the other mound with his hot breath, tongue, and fingers.

Her body was hot, her whispered mantra of one name, *Jac*, took over her cognition. She was close to release, but it was just out of her reach. Jac would know just what to do, so she did what she imagined he would do. He would pull her nipple, rolling it into a painful twist. She slipped her finger through her wetness that coated her vaginal wall and outer realm, and then pinched her clit.

She cried out, "Jac," as she froze for a second to ride the first hard wave of orgasm before closing her thighs tightly, moving in cadence to the multiple crashes. Finally, her body relaxed. If thinking of him could climax her so strongly, then how much would she shatter if he was the one behind the teasing? Jac was it for her and he didn't even know or care. She was so screwed.

Getting up and dressing for the day, which for today started after lunch, she decided she had to get her boss out of her mind. She'd thought Jac was going to make a move after the Kyle incident, but he didn't. For a day, he was overly concerned. He was almost like a teen with a crush and then, nothing.

It was a week since she'd had that ordeal. He was as distant as he had ever been and on some days even more. She needed to figure out how to have a life without thinking of him whenever she heard his voice, saw his face, saw a vehicle that looked like his, or had any spare moment not filled with work. Yes, she was entirely screwed. Time to take her life into her own hands. Becky didn't think it was a good idea, but she would always back Sharlee's endeavors. She was a good friend.

Chapter 10

"What the hell are you doing?"

Sharlee closed out her screen fast. She looked over her shoulder, and up into Garrett's horrified face, and froze. *She should have closed the door. Dummy. Act cool. It's no big deal. It's no big deal.* Sharlee gave Garrett a confused look. At least she hoped it was a confused look.

The two other men in the room, her other self-appointed bosses, looked in her direction trying to assess what Garrett was so upset about. She looked in the direction she expected to see Jac. She breathed a sigh of relief when she didn't see him in his office. Now if she could just slow her galloping heart.

Sharlee wasn't sure why she'd done it, but she had; she'd hit send on her computer. It had been an inner challenge to find a way to forget her feelings for Jac and she knew it was now or never. At that moment however, as Garrett caught a glimpse of something on the screen, maybe the name of the company, all of her previous panic was hyped again, questioning her own judgment. It was not the best scenario, but hey, a girl had to do something, right? *Right?*

It wasn't as though she hadn't had those uneasy feelings before when thinking about this whole mess, but now she'd committed herself. Well, not committed exactly, she'd just agreed to consider a short-term obligation. She could always say no.

Finally, she was more than just contemplating gaining a cyber pal, but she was actually doing it. Maybe.

Her heart wasn't in it, but she needed a date, and these guys forced her to do it. In a way. Kinda. Who was she kidding? She'd rather curl up with Jac and forget the party altogether, but she wasn't Cinderella, and she didn't get the prince after the ball was over. She was his employee who garnered most of his attention while over his knee staring at the floor. Reviewing the computer application, she said she was "adventurous" and "open to exploration" in the relationship department but that sex was not a given. When was it ever? Not that she hadn't wanted it, but it had been a long time since she had wanted it with anyone who shared her desires and attraction, besides Jac.

"Um, what are you talking about?" Sharlee asked as she perused some of her surveillance feeds on their various clients. She turned to check her facial recognition program as it ran an unknown through its data base.

Garrett Sullivan was like the other guys: tough, protective, full of testosterone and one hunk of a man with no filter when it came to her. Now, with his Callie having left town suddenly, he was even more aggressively reactive to her situations. She was a fully functioning member of the team until times like this, when she became a girl with a ton of brothers.

Brothers who wouldn't understand her trouble finding a date because they could find one in ten minutes on any given day. Men who would never understand that the difficulty she had finding a good date wasn't simply because women had to be more careful in their selection. She had to stop comparing the man she wants to the men she is trying to substitute. Maybe that was the problem. It was not possible to do a substitution.

Garrett's sable brown hair was thick and straight. It was a little long and framed his classical features which included an almost perfect nose and chin, and eyes the oddest color of blue she'd ever seen. They almost looked purple at times, like now. Those unique eyes that could see through her smoke screen were staring at her now trying to do just that. Monroe and the rest had their own wow factors without effort, and she didn't even know how to put on makeup very well.

Sharlee was good at what she did and that was hiding. She could live behind a nearly impenetrable wall for as long as she had to. That included hiding from the reality of commitment in her private life and a man she wanted, but who didn't feel the same need for her. Actually, she had plenty of significant men in her life so what was she really looking for? A cyber friend to do the "quasi, virtual boyfriend" gig until needed but when the event was over, in this case the office Christmas party, she'd be done, and he could vanish into thin air. In fact, that would be preferable.

Now that she thought about it in the light of having been discovered, she worried she'd lost all reality. It would never work. Besides, any man who came to an event with her would find himself traumatized by the end of the affair. The guys were ruthless. Mark was the devil incarnate, Carter would try to intimidate him and unless she chose Godzilla's brother, it would be inevitable that Carter would win.

Monroe would ask anything, and sensitivity had no part in it if he wanted an answer. It could make her feel special, at times, but didn't help her find a long-term guy. Not that she wanted one since the Kyle incident. Not really. Hell, she wanted Jac. Maybe she could show him that she was desirable to other men and then make him jealous or interested, anyway. She was going to take the chance. Maybe.

Garrett stared at her and then lowered his voice. "Sharlee, you didn't put your information in that system, did you?"

"Garrett, what are you talking about? I'm the expert, remember?"

"That dating service. Tell me you did not put your name in that slime infested system."

"No, I was just looking, but I've done my research. There are a few sites that are legitimate."

"You wouldn't lie to me would you, little girl?"

"Probably, but I'm not." She laughed.

Both Garrett and Monroe talked to her and treated her as though she was their underage, errant little sister and they still needed to stand guard over her innocence. Well the virginity ship had sailed: twice while in college, a long time ago, but it had sailed. Yep, she was nearly an innocent outside of a few awkward make out sessions since college. Even without the guys' diligence she was not getting regular sex.

She'd touted that she'd not be one of the thousands who found her soul mate through www.feelinginadequate.com or whatever the flavor of the month was called. Besides, she just needed a date, really. And all this trouble was because she'd made a stupid bet.

She'd said she'd bring a date for the Christmas get together after appearing the first year without one. She would have to bring them her kitchen sink cookies every month for a year if she didn't. If they lost, they took her to breakfast every month for a year.

Then there came the secondary wager between the guys. It seemed more enticing to these Neanderthals than the original one. The second money pot emerged when Mark Jensen, usually the more silent of the male orangutans, said she would renege on the first bet. She soon learned that men were so competitive, they'd lay money on anything.

Sharlee was an intelligent woman with plenty to offer. She simply had no real takers. Ever. But that was fine, really, during the spring and even early fall, summer was hard because people were out and doing things. Going stag wasn't the best-case scenario when everyone else had a date. But holiday parties were the worst. Even her parents gave her a little push back then.

Mid-October through mid-February sucked. That time of year was so painful they brought with them a physical ache. Well, this next Christmas was nearly two years with these guys, and she was going to have a date for the office Christmas party this year come hell or high water. But it had to be someone confident and intelligent.

She was well known for superior intelligence in the world of computers, cyber infiltrations into the dark side of the deepest web connections in all its hidden mystery, and her infamous single status. She had two months before the Christmas party and by golly, she was going to get a date for that damn shindig, get happy on as much alcohol as she could sneak past the guys, and shut everyone up. Stuff this computer dating site.

This year she was going to do the party with Jac as her present. It was going to take some planning, that's all. It would surprise them all, especially Jac. He was avoiding her most of the time and Becky was right. She shouldn't let him get away with that. Women went after what they wanted all the time. Just because she hadn't and didn't even know how, shouldn't stop her. Nope. He was going to be under siege but with no defenses.

"You do know that I can get into their system, do whatever I want and get out without leaving a trace, right?" She was smug about her abilities.

"But you didn't, right?" said Monroe in a chastising voice, his eyebrow lifted for affect.

"No I didn't hack their system. There'd be no challenge. I was just looking, okay. You're not the boss of my private life." If she had any.

A voice emanated from behind them both. A deep, gravelly voice that sent shivers climbing her spine every time. The voice of the man she wanted to be the boss of her whole life, private, public and everything in between. The man got her attention every time but for now, only featured every night as her personal orgasm buddy.

"Sweetheart, none of us has a private life that's *that* private. We watch each other's backs, always. Now, promise me you didn't put your information on anything that would compromise you or us."

She could answer that truthfully because it was a pseudo life with pseudo everything. "No sir, I did not."

Jacquard smiled. "Good girl." He pointed to her face recognition screens. "Now tell me what we have going here."

She wanted to stick her tongue out at Garrett who still seemed hesitant to let things go but he did. Sharlee launched into explaining where she was on the newest work and everyone else went back to doing whatever they were doing.

That night, Charlotte snuggled under her fuzzy throw on her sofa as she was keeping an eye on the surveillance cameras they had set up for a client. Out of the corner of her eye, she noticed some activity in the back of the house. Don't be paranoid Charlotte. It's probably nothing. Her lights didn't blink, and her alert didn't go off. She took a few notes for review by the guys tomorrow. You couldn't be too careful with a senator.

Her job on the team was to get the intel. Theirs was to figure out what to do with it. She'd learned that lesson well. She could lose herself in cyber-space not to be found until she decided it was time and then she could evaporate again. That is why her code name was Vapor. She was a cyber mist and nothing more.

She used her skill to search around for background on Kyle. She found some information and wondered if she should share it but since it was only a hunch, she thought she would check it out herself and then share. Jac wouldn't be happy if he found out, but she didn't have to share with him how long it took to get the information. Just that she had it.

Kyle apparently had been hired by the same client she was just watching on CCTV and one she had personally held a contract for recently. It was an interesting connection but could easily be coincidental. There was another odd thing involving email, Kyle, her, and some unknown entity. She needed to see if she could tie some of the loose ends together before she let the guys in on her information.

Remembering what had happened the last time she'd gone out to investigate, she assured her troubled mind and butt that it was her hometown. If she wanted to visit it, there should be no complaints. Except there would be. Of that fact, she had no doubt. That is if they discovered why she was there. The best attack is one that they didn't see coming and the best way to get out of Jacquard Reynaud's line of fire was to make sure he knew beforehand.

He would never know what hit him.

Chapter 11

Sharlee started her shut down procedures. She was dead on her feet. She locked up her computer in the vault Jac had put in her apartment wall and stood to stretch. She'd been monitoring two sets of cameras. The first group was the senator's place. The second set was an operation that came out at night, so she was up until the sun greeted her and then she tried to go down for a few hours' sleep, but she was grumpy.

That happened as often as not, operating on a little sleep. She didn't have to monitor every job, but if she was going to be up anyway... She was almost done with her part of the intelligence gathering. Time to call it a day and go to bed, as soon as she made some breakfast of Sugar X's and O's, her favorite cereal. What a play on the very thing that she didn't have in her life, hugs, and kisses.

As she yawned again and crunched on the cereal, she wondered, not for the first time, if she was her own worst enemy living here. Maybe she should move out of this crazy metropolitan whirlwind and find a little town with good potential. She could and often did, do her job wherever in the world she was. Maybe she could convince them that since she could do her job at home, only coming in twice a week was enough.

She could keep her contract jobs and do them in Anywhere, USA if she wanted to. Her research and intelligence gathering didn't have borders or boundaries. She often thought of relocation when she was discontent, or when she remembered how hopeless it was to dream of Jac acting on or even acknowledging his feelings for her. She needed sleep.

One reason she hesitated was the pay. It was unbelievable, the benefits were incredible, and she got to keep her side jobs. Who was she kidding? If she could get Jac to pay attention to her, consistently, then she would stay for free.

They were always on-call designation. It was a nice way of saying, 'we call, you answer.' Only it was harder for her, who worked half the night, only to be called in to make an 8 a.m. mandatory meeting Jac just thought up. Sharlee told Kaden that she should sleep with her boots on and laughed. Now, when they had something that could go down at any moment, *boots* was their code for be ready, it's about to hit the fan. She was expected to respond much like her teammates except stay inside.

She knew that if she needed anything they were there in a flash. Unfortunately, they were just as quick if she made a bad judgement call. Tomorrow, she thought as she dozed off, maybe she'd check on the dating site one more time tomorrow, before closing it all down, but now it was time to get as many minutes of sleep as she could.

Miraculously, when she woke up a few hours later, Sharlee remembered her thoughts the night before. She did a quick check on the dating site. There were many who had sent messages, but as she closed the last profile Sharlee knew she wasn't even curious about any of them.

Jac was what she wanted. She would just go after him. She was as wishy washy as he was. First, she decided to pursue him then she backed off only to decide to try again. Jac was exactly the same. He had given her signs he was interested but then had backed off. With a heavy sigh, she deleted her online profile with renewed determination.

She had a lot to do. Charlotte started her day, tired though she was, plotting and planning that man's demise. With a new objective in her days, life became more fun. Jacquard Reynaud didn't know what was going on, but Monroe and Garrett caught on fast and had given her the nod to continue.

"Within reason," said Garrett sternly.

"Even if I could, I'm not going to hurt the man. I'm just going to show him what he is missing and what it would look like if he experienced us."

"I don't think knowing what he's missing is the problem."

She'd show up in Jac's office instead of buzzing him to let him know about all manner of work-related things. This morning's results told her she was on the right track.

Walking into Jac's office, she went around and stood next to him to show him some stills of the man they were keeping an eye on.

"Why bring these in? You could've just sent them by email, like you usually do."

She shrugged. "I had to print something else so since I know you like printouts of the pictures for the wall, I thought I would save Becky a step."

It had never dawned on her until that very moment but maybe he wanted to have his office manager print it because he enjoyed her company, sought out her company. An unprecedented feeling of jealousy raced through her body and she immediately squelched it. Becky was her friend and had recently discovered she was attracted to Carter.

"Unless you would rather I leave these for her."

His hand was warm as it covered hers on the desk. "No, I prefer you every time."

They stood looking at each other until Kaden knocked on the open door and the time that had slowed and shrunk to encompass only Sharlee and Jac suddenly expanded to the rest of reality.

"I've lots to do today, Charlotte, but if you need me for anything, call. Promise me."

"I'm fine but if that changes I'll call."

Jac was beginning to respond to her overtures. She was drawing closer instead of fighting to keep the space between them and it was working. He was lowering his guard and letting her in slowly, but she needed to do something new to keep him off balance. She had an idea.

As she left Jac to his work, she began scheming. If the way to a man's heart is through his stomach, she could work that angle and use the guys to help without them even knowing. She knew for a fact that Jac had a sweet tooth that he rarely fed because of the calories. He was the one who usually sprang for lunch. She would feed his craving while hopefully creating another.

Pursuing a relationship with him was kind of fun. She grabbed Becky to help her that night.

Sharlee entered the office at lunchtime the next day to cheers.

"Hey, Sharlee brought lunch!" yelled the always hungry Carter as he and Mark walked in the office behind her.

"I'm surprised you waited this long for lunch, Carter."

"I had a snack a little while ago."

Mark snorted. "Yeah, his snack was at the 'all you can eat' pancake house."

Sharlee rolled her eyes as everyone else laughed.

She laid out the food on the counter before grabbing her own sub and going to her office.

She'd bought a veggie sub for herself and Becky, but she made them put lean turkey or roast beef on everyone else's because she knew her guys wouldn't touch them without meat. She'd made low fat raspberry cheesecake because it was Jac's favorite. She added dark chocolate brownies, another of his favorites, before she quit baking the night before. To that she'd added two large bags of low sodium chips, and bottles of spring water.

"Hey, they forgot the meat on mine," yelled Garrett.

"No, it just has veggies too," she yelled back.

His response was silence.

Mark peeked into her office, "Thanks for lunch, Sharlee," he said, but his enthusiasm had dampened.

"You're welcome," she answered as she followed him back into the central office area on her way to the employee break room. As Monroe looked up and saw her enter, he said, "Hey, I think you grabbed the wrong type of chips, but they aren't that bad, really."

"Good. And I didn't grab the wrong bag, and they didn't forget your meat. You guys eat too much junk. Once in a while you need someone to take care of you. Those bimbos you hang out with aren't going to do it, so I figure it's up to me. So, if you want cheesecake and brownies, you had better eat your lunch without grumbling."

Garrett laughed. "I'm from California so I've had my fill of hippie food, but I'll let a woman take care of me anytime she wants." Sharlee smiled at him and knew he missed his girlfriend Katrina. She did too now that she had left. Sharlee wished there was something she could do for him, but she had to concentrate on her own love life first.

Jac had walked quietly into the office behind Sharlee standing in the entrance of the too small lunchroom. She jumped when he spoke.

"I figure it means a few less reps in evening PT so hand it over sweetheart."

Turning, she smiled and handed him a sandwich but his eyes, so warm and inviting, drew her into their depths. "I'll bring you some raspberry cheesecake in a little while."

"That would be perfect... If you had a piece with me."

She nodded. "Have you had too much coffee, or do you want some when I bring in the dessert?"

"Love some."

Kaden broke in, not noticing the two standing in the middle of the room were dancing with their words and looks. "I don't mind this. Hey Sharlee, I could get used to vegetables on my sandwich." He was bombarded with wadded up sub wrappings.

Sharlee grimaced and then laughed as she looked away from Jacquard. Kaden always had the worst timing.

"Good to know, Kaden. I'll try to help you out when I can." When she turned back, Jac was gone.

That's okay, Jacquard Reynaud. You can run, and you can hide, but I'll always find you.

Eating her raspberry cheesecake with Jac made everything more intense. They ate in silence, but the way he watched her open her mouth to receive the sweet made her wiggle in her arousal. Watching Jac wrap his tongue around the fork to remove the last taste of raspberry was her undoing. She moaned, and he smiled wickedly.

She'd added a large brownie to Jac's plate, but she wouldn't last another confection. Sharlee rose to leave, and he stood, coming to stand in front of her. Without a word, he leaned down and licked the corner of her lips, savoring the residue before kissing her gently.

"Thank you for lunch and dessert, Charlotte. I'll have to return the favor when there isn't an audience."

"I'd love that." Jac stepped back and Sharlee returned to her office wondering if she would be able to get any work done.

Lunch over, she accepted the team's thanks as they left for other assignments. That left Sharlee to spend the afternoon watching video until she decided to call it a night. She was glad there was no night surveillance and just a couple of hours left of reviewing the senator's feeds. She was tired. She had gotten Jac to agree to giving her a few days off.

"I need a break, Jac."

"Fine, I'll go with you."

"No, I can go by myself."

"I know you can, but if you want an actual break, let me show you the cabin I own in the mountains. It will take your breath away and you will relax."

"Sounds heavenly but can I get a raincheck?"

Jac hesitated. Jac always paused before agreeing if he wanted something else. "Raincheck."

"Can I leave tomorrow? I'll be back Monday."

Jac nodded "See you Monday."

She grinned and barely stopped herself from hugging him. "Thanks, Jac. I'll make it up to you."

He simply nodded and went back to work. For once, Sharlee was glad Jac didn't encourage her to stick around. The less time she spent in his company, the better. She didn't lie to him, but she wasn't as forthcoming as she should be but she couldn't risk Jac asking too many questions.

Chapter 12

After Sharlee got home, she went right to work on the last of her review work because she was fading fast. Finally satisfied, she stood under a hot, relaxing shower, and devoured the second half of her foot-long veggie sub. Feeling dead on her feet, she sipped a cup of chamomile tea while reading on her tablet in bed. She turned off the light knowing she'd drop off to sleep quickly. If she'd been less exhausted, Sharlee knew she would have had a difficult time going to sleep. Her head was full of thoughts about how she was going to handle tomorrow, but weariness overcame all else.

The next morning, Sharlee threw a few clothes and essentials into her SUV and headed for her hometown to speak to Kyle's mother. She'd called Mrs. Martin before she left Lexington and asked a couple of questions. Evidently, Kyle had spoken to his mother about Sharlee.

"I always thought he had a little crush on you, but I guess it never progressed." His mother sounded sad and yet spoke with a modicum of hope.

"No Mrs. Martin, it never went further than that. We were friends until, well, anyway, he sent you emails from my account." Okay it wasn't technically true, but she was sure Mrs. Martin wouldn't know that.

"Really dear? I didn't get any emails from your address. I guess they went into a *spam* something. I never found out what that was, really. Not food, anyway. And I don't think I've gotten an email from Kyle in months."

Bingo. The emails Sharlee had found in her deep search that he was sending to his mother were obviously not to his mother's account. Or maybe they went to that elusive spam folder. What was he up to? A couple of the emails insinuated there was a closer bond to Sharlee than she liked. This was her chance to get more information without jeopardizing anyone finding out.

"Mrs. Martin, I'm going to be in town tonight. Do you think I could find those emails for you? I could do some computer maintenance and make your email easier to use."

"Oh, would you dear? That would be wonderful. How about I cook you dinner as payment?"

"You don't have to do that."

"Please, I have other computer questions and it would be my way of paying you."

"I would love a home cooked meal. It's no fun to cook for one and I would love to catch up while I fiddle with cleaning up your email."

"It's a date."

"Good. See you soon."

The dear woman never once questioned why Sharlee, who no longer lived in town, would spend her first night there helping with her email and answering general computer questions. She was an easy target for Kyle to use her email as an access point in his dirty dealings.

As she drove in the direction of Memphis and away from the Lexington, Friday morning traffic, there was a peacefulness that came over her. Kentucky was a beautiful state. She loved it like she loved her home state of Tennessee. Lexington was smaller than Memphis by half, but the character of the place was huge.

All the way along the interstate, she saw the reoccurrence of a little non-descript blue car. Of course, it could have just been someone going in the same direction. It did feel odd when she stopped for the bathroom about halfway through her trip. When she pulled back onto the road, it wasn't long before the car reappeared a short distance behind her. She almost called Jac, but he couldn't have done anything, and it was just a co-incidence. That thought solidified when she pulled off for gas near Memphis and she didn't see the car again.

However, as she pulled into the Martin driveway, she no-ticed the car parked on the street. She chastised herself for al-lowing silly things like similar cars showing up to unnerve her. No matter how she tried to blow it off, she couldn't, and again, she almost called Jac. She stared at the vehicle trying to decide if she should call him or ignore it. Mrs. Martin called her from the door of the house, breaking into her thoughts. Sharlee gave one final mental head shake and climbed out of her car. She made a deliberate move to turn around and stare at the car. If they were following her it was now known that she had spotted them. If they weren't-no harm.

"Charlotte, come inside. It's getting chilly tonight, dear."

Charlotte smiled. Fifty-five degrees was not very chilly, but she smiled and did as she was bid. She grabbed her gear, looking back before going inside. The car was gone. Maybe she was just paranoid.

"Thanks for inviting me, Mrs. Martin."

"Call me Helen."

Helen had offered for Sharlee to stay the night and while she hadn't planned on it, it was better than a hotel. Sharlee didn't tell Jac that her parents, Trudy and Grant Armstrong, lived in Florida now, not Memphis. He didn't ask and since she never mentioned visiting her parents, it wasn't a lie. Except something about omission came to her mind before it dissolved in the warmth of Helen's welcome.

By the time she started back to her apartment the next afternoon, Sharlee had come away with more questions than answers. She explained to Helen there was trouble with her email.

There was, with the new one in her name but she didn't own. So as Sharlee worked on changing the new and existing email access and security, Helen said she didn't need two emails. It made sense, so while Sharlee said she was deleting the one that Helen had no access to, she renamed it to her childhood dog's name.

Then she changed the routing and access codes and did some fancy diversion so not only would it not connect Helen to her son's mess, disconnected him from it as of now, and in a very scrambled way, diverted it to her childhood dog aka Sharlee.

Yes, it was wrong, and yes, she should have felt guilty, but she didn't. The security questions were set up with Helen's real-life answers, so it was easy to complete the switch. Mrs. Martin was happy, Charlotte was happy, and Kyle had proven, once again, what a moron he really was. He even had the confirmation security email for the fake account going to his mother's authentic account.

She could now intercept the emails without removing from the server so the intended receiver still received them without notice. She cleaned up all of Helen's emails and system, set it up for easy access and left. As she drove out of town, she could have sworn she saw the same car follow her but shook it off. *Charlotte, you sound like the guys. Paranoid. No one is following you.* But as she continued, she couldn't shake it off and so she finally called Jac.

"I think someone is following me."

"Damn. Why do you think so?"

"Well, they were behind me when I drove in, and they parked at the house when I stopped. Now they've been behind me for close to two hundred miles."

"Damn sweetheart. And you are just calling me? We will talk about that later. Where are you?"

"I just passed Princeton."

"Okay. I need you to go back to Princeton. I have a cousin there that will keep you safe until I arrive."

"No, I just wanted you to know. And besides, I think I can shake them."

"Listen to me little girl—"

She knew hanging up on Jac was going to bite her in the ass, but she wanted to get home. She waited until there was more traffic and changed lanes until she was on the far inside lane of the interstate. What she called the haul ass lane. Then she planned her move carefully and held her breath as she cut in front of several cars to take the exit quickly. Without advance notice, the driver of the car following her couldn't change lanes fast enough in all the traffic, and he missed the turn.

Charlotte knew the area well enough to take a back way for a few miles and then cut back onto the interstate. She didn't see the tail again that night. When she arrived home, Jac was waiting along with Kaden.

"Don't say it. I lost my tail right after I got off the phone with you, so I must have been mistaken."

"You mean when you hung up on me."

"Did I? Sorry. I'm tired and want to go to bed."

Charlotte headed into the elevator and two bulky men followed her. Why did she ever think she could do anything they wouldn't find out about? After they arrived at Sharlee's apartment, the place was checked for any signs of disruption but there didn't appear to be any. The little telltale things Sharlee had placed around before leaving were all still undisturbed.

"Hey, you have a message. I wonder who would have left you a message. I mean it wouldn't have been your parents because you were just home? We would call your cell. So would most of your friends, right? We'd better check." Kaden hit the play button.

"Hey, dear. Sorry we missed you. I know you're busy but on your next break, maybe you could come see us. You always say your work goes anywhere. Okay, well, call when you can, we are both healthy. Love you."

Charlotte sat down hard on the armchair. "Was that your mother, Charlotte?" Jac was calm.

"Mm, yes."

"You lied to me."

"No, I did go to Memphis."

"But not to see your parents."

"I never mentioned them once." Yes, that was true so why was her heart pounding, her stomach flipping and her ass twitching?

"Omission is still a lie."

"I'm not a child, Jac. I needed to go to Memphis but not to see my parents. You filled in the blank the way you wanted to." Her belligerence was heard loudly.

He ignored her statement. "Was it worth it?"

"Of course, now I'll have the inside track I needed."

"Good. Just remember the sneakiness was worth the payment demanded."

"You aren't spanking me, Jac. You have decided you don't have the right by ignoring me at all other times. I didn't do anything wrong."

"It's late. We'll talk about it tomorrow, first thing. Kaden is spending the night."

He ignored her words again. It was so infuriating. "I'm not going back to work until Monday. And Kaden is not spending the night."

"Your leave is cancelled."

"Dammit Jac, it's Saturday."

"Tomorrow, nine o'clock."

"I won't be there."

Jack stepped close. "Oh, I think you will, little girl, if you know what's good for you."

She creamed, and tingled, and wanted to be left alone so she could take care of the ache.

"No Kaden."

"Fine, no Kaden."

"Goodnight."

Kaden walked into the hallway.

Before she had any idea it was coming, Jac kissed her. Hard. "Tomorrow, Charlotte. No excuses."

She didn't answer but locked the door and set the alarm. Lord she needed her vibrator or a cold shower, maybe both.

Chapter 13

Charlotte jerked awake. The screaming in her ears was so loud. Her heart was pounding out of her chest. Did she have a nightmare? Her sleep was so deep it was hard to know what it was. Her eyes could hardly open. Her head was fuzzy. She couldn't read the clock. Hell and damnation, as her grandfather was known to say, what was wrong with her? Was her morning alarm going off in this darkness? Winter made it so hard to tell the time of day.

Finally identifying the shrill noise as her house alarms going off, not her morning alarm, she threw the blanket off her tank and shorts encased body to take care of it. Now her cell was ringing. She knocked it off the table in an attempt to get at it. Snatching the phone off the floor, she saw the call came from Kaden. It was Kaden's week for emergency responses. She redialed him as she went to reset the alarm.

"Kaden, what the hell is going on? Who tripped my alarm?"

"Sharlee, is someone in your house?" He wasn't playing, and this wasn't a drill.

"Um, I don't think so. I was sleeping." She reset the alarm and checked the door. "The lock is still engaged."

"Dead bolted, too?"

She checked. "No," came her dejected answer.

"But you locked it after we left last night, right?"

"I think so. Who would want to be in my apartment? I don't have anything."

"Who have you brought to your place?"

"Lots of people."

"What? How many?"

"Shut up. No one, only you guys. I have no life, remember?"

"Okay. Enough. You have to help me here. I've checked all the rooms and don't see anyone. I haven't had time to review the digital surrounding the tripping of the alarm, but I will. Stay on the phone with me until Mark shows up."

"I don't need a babysitter and what do you mean you checked all the rooms? How?"

Out came the voice she had heard Kaden use with his girlfriend when he was irritated with her on the phone. The tone of voice that would have sunk into her own bones if it were Jac speaking to her like that.

"Listen to me. It's your safety and I am not budging on this. Do not go against me, Charlotte."

Charlotte. Okay then. "Yeah, all right." He was only a year older than she was but right now, he might have been ten years older.

"Good girl. Now, if you're too flimsy dressed, you might want to throw on something before Mark gets there, which will be in about four minutes."

"God, I hate you guys sometimes. If you are treating me like your little sister, I shouldn't have to dress up for you to come over."

"Suit yourself. Personally, I like that little outfit."

"How the..." She swore a blue streak as she put the phone on speaker and put on a pair of sweats and a tee shirt.

"He's there. Nine minutes, that's a new record." She rolled her eyes and reached for the door not wanting to know why they had a best time established from their houses or the office to her apartment.

"Don't open the door," admonished Kaden.

"Have I said I hated you lately?"

Kaden laughed. "I'm sure you did and will again. Wait until he knocks."

"Why doesn't he just open it with his key?"

"You know about that?"

"Hell and damnation, I hate you all." She hung up on Kaden. If Mark was here, then she didn't need to wait on the line any longer. She slammed into the kitchen to make coffee. When the phone rang again, she let it go to voicemail.

She had the coffee brewing and bacon in the pan before Mark knocked on the door. He must have done some reconnaissance before coming up. She opened it. "Next time use your key."

"Well, good morning to you too. Who told you about the key?"

"I guessed and I'm not sure I would call this morning good since I didn't go to sleep until four hours ago."

"Nah, that's lots of sleep. Okay, so have you looked everywhere?"

"No, I had to change into decent clothes so you didn't see me in my pjs that Kaden thought might be too risqué. You were supposed to be at my door a full five minutes ago. Get lost from the parking lot?"

"Right." Mark ignored her question and systematically looked in every room before reappearing in the kitchen. "It's all clear now, anyway. I'll work on the entries and exits as soon as I get some of that coffee and Kaden lets me know what he found on the tapes. You tell me what someone might want from your apartment."

"Nothing. There isn't anything anyone would want in here, well, sleep might be nice."

"You're really nasty today, huh?"

"Yeah well, I had a hard few days, and I didn't sleep because, well, I don't know why. Then I worked on the new assignment until I couldn't do it any longer. I was up until almost two before falling asleep only to be woken up by a blaring alarm system and a screaming cell phone. Then I had a bossy man dictate to me what I should do before I got my needed coffee and food. Then another one showed up, refused to answer my questions and searched my house. So yeah, I'm feeling nasty. What took you so long?"

"Ah, there's the coffee, the elixir of the gods. I didn't get enough yet today. And on my way up here, I was intercepted by someone outside the elevators, he got away but not before I got him in the surveillance camera."

"What surveillance camera?"

"The one we installed to watch the parking lot at the bottom of the elevator."

"Of course." Sharlee slammed the heavy coffee cup on the counter.

Garrett and Jac walked in. Charlotte greeted them. "So nice of you to join the party." Mark shook his head at the other two in warning and Charlotte caught it. "Yes, I'm in a mood."

She had added more bacon and poured coffee as the men conferred with each other before she thought of the safe.

"Damn." Walking into her little dining area, she visually examined the outer wall. It appeared normal. Opening the wall panel door that hid the safe, she looked at the dial on the closed safe. It was on forty. Someone had been tampering with it.

"Jac, someone has been here."

"I thought we'd crossed that bridge, but why do you say that?" asked Mark once again alert.

"The dial is on forty." The men waited until she finished. "I always leave it at seven. Always."

"Are you sure?" asked Garrett.

"What does, 'I always leave it on seven' mean? I'm not a moron."

Jac came up behind Sharlee. "Watch it sweetheart, my hand is getting awfully itchy."

She graced him with a nasty look. "Yes, I set it on seven at night and check to make sure it is on that number in the morning. This is the first morning it hasn't been on the right number."

"Maybe you were tired. You were up until early this morning," offered Mark.

"Stop it. I'm not a child. It's a purposeful habit. Like brushing my teeth. I do it the same way every day. I could do it in my sleep."

Garrett sat down and stared at the open panel but said nothing. Jac strolled through her two-bedroom apartment and finally sat in the living room, also silent. The apartment was roomy, but it was positively matchbook size with three large men inside it. Mark pulled out a kit and took a chance that he could get fingerprints off the safe.

Charlotte scrambled eggs, throwing them on her only serving platter with the bacon. Next, she promptly dropped her coffee cup, spilling coffee everywhere. As if on cue, her tears flowed as she tried to see through the waterfall to grab a kitchen towel to clean up the mess. All three men were on high alert but only one grabbed Sharlee. That man was Jac. He picked her up and moved her from the kitchen.

The other two, as if waiting for Jac to move, cleaned the mess quietly and efficiently as Jac led the crying woman into her bedroom. Sitting in her large armchair, he pulled her onto his lap and held her tightly while she decompressed. Soon her tears were replaced by anger, and she tried to get out of Jac's lap. "Settle woman. I need to talk to you." She continued to fight him.

He slapped her flank.

She stopped her efforts to get up.

"Are you ready to listen?"

"Do I have a choice?" She was sassy and irritated. "In anything?"

Jac chuckled. "Good point. Well, you do have a choice how you hear me, from this spot or over my knee examining the carpet."

Sharlee sniffed but settled back into her place on his lap. Jack kissed her temple. "Well-chosen. I need you to pack your things and come to my place."

Sitting up fast, she almost clipped his chin with her head. Sharlee tried unsuccessfully to climb back out of his lap.

"What? No Jac, I'm not running scared from something I don't even know is a threat."

He tapped her nose gently, giving her a stern look. "You're listening, remember?"

Charlotte gave him a sour look but kept quiet. She wanted to stand up but didn't want to disrupt the hold he had on her. She'd dreamed often of sitting like this, in her bedroom, cuddling.

"Okay. Now no one is saying you're scared. I'm saying I can't afford to be worried about you every moment you aren't with one of us."

She sat up. "Jac, it could've been anyone. A fluke, it's likely to have been a fluke."

"Great. But until this place has been swept clean, all tapes have been reviewed, and we're sure it was a random act, you are not staying here. Let me remind you that someone committing a random act wouldn't know where your hidden panel is."

"Right, but I don't want to put you out. I, um, could sleep on your couch in the office."

He shook his head. "Nope."

"You don't worry about the guys when stuff happens with them."

"I do, they buddy up if crap we don't expect happens. But they can kick some serious butt."

"I can too. I'm good."

"And smaller than most men in this business. Sweetheart, I don't know what's going on here. If I did, I'd take care of it, and it would be life back to normal. Except for us. I've had my reservations for a long time and have held off but this time, I'm not refusing what I want. And let there be no mistake, I want you, Charlotte Hope Armstrong."

"You really want me? What does that mean? Over your lap?" Her heart jumped in her chest, and she was afraid to breathe lest it change the outcome. Having waited so long, she was cautious.

"That's one way I will have you, yes. Sweetheart, it'll take a very long time to show you all the ways I want you."

"Oh."

"Charlotte, I'm not easy to be around and I can be overbearing and obnoxious at times." She grinned.

"I take it you've noticed. Right, so no sweet words here because that isn't me. I just want you in my life, in my home, in my bed, and yes, over my lap at times. So baby if that's something you're into exploring then say so. I've wasted enough time trying to ignore my desires. It almost killed me when you started dating that human reject. Then yesterday's scare, and this morning's were too much to ignore."

"Jacquard, Kyle was ages ago and I don't know that yesterday and today aren't just a couple of coincidences. How are we going to work together if we are, you know, together?"

"Much better I hope. Look, we have a good start. We'll negotiate things as they come up. You're into having your ass roasted and I am into roasting it. You set off all my alarms and warnings, and I seem to be drawn to Charlie Foxtrots, so I want to try. I'm not going to say any of the touchy-feely 'right' words here and I'm not going to say it will be easy but as my mother told me a million times, nothing worth having ever is."

"Are you saying I'm a cluster...?

"No, don't put words in my mouth. I'm saying this whole thing is one. Never mind. What do you say, sweetheart?"

"Okay." She nodded once.

"Okay?" His eyebrows rose.

"Okay, we will try it. Okay, I'll go to your place. Okay, we will see if we can work together."

Jac leaned in and his lips hovered just over hers. "Okay then." His kiss started softly, exploring her lips and then moved into a more aggressive tongue invasion.

"Jac, hey. Oh, sorry man, but we've got a situation." Mark was somber.

Jacquard was immediately on alert. He stood, pushing Sharlee behind him before she could process what had happened. She tried to go ahead of him only to feel his arm snaking around her waist and yank her back.

"Stand down, Charlotte."

His look reinforced the message of his words. She looked at Jac and the bedroom door. She took a step away and a step forward. She heard his sigh and saw, out of the corner of her eye, his head shake. Mark had gone back to where he had come from when Jac grabbed her upper arm.

"Sorry, sorry." She sighed. "But it's my apartment."

"And I told you to stand down. I don't intend to repeat my instructions continually. I'm not trying to hide things from you, I'm keeping you safe. Understand?"

She nodded. "Ye-ouch. Ow, Jac, I get it. Ow, okay, stop. Quit smacking my butt. Everyone can hear you. Jac, I'll listen."

"Then hush," was his only response as his message continued for another few seconds.

Charlotte kept silent but with difficulty. She used to think a spanking would take minutes, but she was beginning to have some experience now. She could say with confidence that her man—yes, she could say that now—could do a considerable amount of damage on her posterior in thirty seconds.

As soon as the swats ended, she found herself crushed against his muscular chest and her lips joined with his, his hands lightly squeezing her bottom. Jac fervently kissed her hiss of stinging butt to a whimper followed by a moan before releasing her. He spoke next to her ear. Her breathing became shallower at the timbre of his voice and the implication of his words.

"Do I need to remind you I am still your boss and that now we are in a relationship does not mean you can disobey me? I told you things would be different. You're not just my employee now, you are mine. That position will find you in significantly more hot water than you ever intended to be in if you defy me when I am trying to keep you safe. I have not forgotten we still have yesterday to address."

His face was serious, her lips were bruised, and her bottom was throbbing. "Yes, sir," was her only acceptable response.

Jacquard nodded as he slid his arm around her waist again. "Good girl," he said as she leaned into him, and he kissed her temple.

"Now stay here until I come get you."

Chapter 14

Jac brought Charlotte with him as he approached Garrett who was going over her living room with a fine-tooth comb, otherwise known as an electronic bug detector. Garrett pushed her towards the kitchen with his finger to his lips. Charlotte couldn't believe Jac and Garrett left her standing there instead of including her but as she processed what was going on, she could see why he was also indicating she should be quiet. She nodded and walked into the kitchen to begin clearing things up.

Mark took Jac outside and spoke to him. "We've found cameras wired for sound in the living room and the hallway so far. We need to sweep in the bedroom and bathroom but maybe even out here. Honestly, I wonder if it wasn't here before we put our equipment up."

"No, we did our own sweep beforehand. Are you sure these aren't the ones we put up?"

"Nope because I identified our one in the kitchen going into the living area and ours don't activate unless the alarm goes off."

"These are on continuously?"

"Yup."

"Do you think in the early days, Sharlee could have let someone else in thinking they were part of us?"

"Damn smart on their part if that's the case but that then begs the question, how did they know? She is closed mouthed, normally."

"Good point. I'll ask her after she's gone from the apartment. You and Garrett finish here. Shut it all down and then put our camera on continual feed until we decide how to proceed."

"Gotcha, boss." Mark went inside as Garrett stepped out. Jac stopped to talk to him.

"What's up? I have Mark pulling their cameras and then putting ours on continuous feed. I think we should probably add an additional lock."

"Sounds good." Garrett paused for a moment as though deciding how he would ask the question. "You and Sharlee, you're good? I mean..."

"Are we together? Yes. And we will be good together when things settle down. We'll have issues, and I imagine Sharlee will have plenty of reasons to complain more often than not, about certain... anatomical parts."

Garrett chuckled. "Yeah, it will be difficult for all of us in the beginning. That woman does like her freedom and control. What do you say I take the lead on this one then? It's important to keep a clear head. Better for you and safer for her... parts."

Jacquard laughed. "Agreed."

The men returned inside, Garrett to talk to Mark and Jac to gather Sharlee. Speaking low and forcing her to do the same, he directed her packing. "Grab what you need for a while. Anything personal you need to keep, grab it too because you won't be back soon."

"But why?" she whispered back.

"We can talk when we're in the car."

"Jac, what about my computer in the safe? We haven't opened it yet."

"I know. Finish. Any prints Mark could've gotten are lifted. I'll stand over you, so the combination isn't compromised any more in case we haven't gotten all the cameras. This is the one time I wish you had a smaller apartment."

"Good thinking on the combination."

"Let's worry about that later. Empty the contents."

"Jac, I don't like the way this sounds."

"Pack and let me worry about the rest. I have some things I need you to do."

"But—" Charlotte's words were cut off by lips descending to touch hers in a hard kiss.

She licked her lips and smiled as his voice came across full of emotional gravel.

"Do not question me right now Charlotte. I think you know I'm not in the mood to take it well. Trust me to know what I'm doing. The next time, my answer won't be a kiss; it'll be more smacks to that delectable ass. Now move it."

Sharlee opened her mouth and Jac's eyes widened before he grew a salacious grin. She gave him a disgusted look and stomped away to pack.

She was a brat, pure and simple. He knew just what to do with a brat, but he wasn't just putting her off when he said they had things to do. He couldn't do the lesson justice right now and he wouldn't deal half-assed on anything to do with his Charlotte. Yep, his. He knew he should have more reservations, and it was entirely possible he would later, but right now it felt right to plow ahead and worry about the straightness of the furrows later.

Once in the car, Jac tossed the bags in the back, placing her computer next to them. The guys would bring all the equipment, hers and the company's, when they came. Sharlee didn't care for that fact.

He held the door for her. "Jac, I want to bring my own equipment. It's my apartment and my things so it is my choice."

Jac said nothing. He reached over and buckled her seatbelt.

She huffed and pushed him out of the way. He tweaked her nipple hard enough to watch as it tightened in response. She pushed harder and placed her arm over her breasts. He slapped it down.

"That is punishment for pouting, so no soothing."

Her look was cautiously guilty with a little play on wounded that he thought was adorable. He leaned in kissing her lightly at first, finding he couldn't release her lips until he had done the job thoroughly. As he settled into his seat and started the car, he grilled Charlotte about anyone who had ever been to her apartment. "Start from the beginning."

"You know, the cable guy, the manager, the electrician that checked the wiring, you guys—"

"What electrician?"

"He said he was there to examine the wiring because there had been a short in the last electrical storm. He was checking for possible problems."

"How long ago was that?"

"I don't know exactly. Oh, about the time I ran into Kyle, probably."

"Did you watch what he did?"

"No, I went to work."

"And left him alone in your place?" he asked with a touch of incredulity.

She answered defensively. "Yes, I mean, we had several big contracts going, and I still had some small ones. I was really busy. I might have asked to stay home, but I was positive the boss might not have liked it."

Jac could appreciate his Charlotte was trying to lighten the mood, but it was lost on him. This was serious, and he hoped his face showed his thoughts.

"Anyway, I figured I couldn't afford to put off some of the work, so I told him to lock up when he was done. Everything was in order when I got home."

"Anything else?" His tone sounded ominous.

"Um, oh, I forgot. The manager sent the maintenance guy over about three months after I moved in, I think, to ask if there was anything that needed fixing. He said there was a light outside my door that needed replacing. He would just check on things and step out."

"And I suppose you let him in alone, too?"

"Yes. But he had a uniform shirt on. I had to go out, so I didn't see a problem."

"Damn. And you say it was about three months after you moved in?"

"About."

"That was right after we put in our equipment."

"Yes and about that." She turned towards him, "You knew there were cameras in my place without my knowledge. Not cool, Jac."

"Everyone gets that. We leave the bathroom and bedroom alone but every place else has some kind of listening device or camera."

"Does Becky know?" Jac was silent. "Why didn't you tell me?"

"You would have thrown a fit, and I didn't want you to quit. Now you know. Your apartment is small enough for two cameras. And while we could manually activate them if we had needed to, the alarm going off activates them automatically. It's a damn good thing we did it, too."

"You don't get to use today as a reason to justify violating my privacy and keeping it a secret from me. In case you can't tell, I'm pretty pissed at you right now. All of you."

"Yeah, Mark said you were testy. But now it's obvious we aren't the only ones with that surveillance idea. Now there are two questions: Who. And how many."

"And why."

"If we know who then we will probably know why. We're going to alert whoever it is because we're taking it down and stripping the room."

"Why don't you leave them? If I'm not going to be there what does it matter? Then you don't tip your hand."

"Sweetheart, our hand has been tipped because I'm sure they know we discovered them today. They were watching, remember? Is there anything else you haven't told us?"

"Is there anything else you haven't told me?"

"Probably, but right now we're going back to the office to find out why you're so interesting."

"Jac, I need to go back and finish cleaning up the place. I can't just leave it for who knows how long. Besides, my lease comes up next month and I need to have it nice so they will renew the lease. They inspect every six months."

"Who does the inspection, the apartment manager?"

"Well, now that the manager is off site, they've been sending a contract company."

"What the hell? Do not tell me that you have been letting someone who isn't the manager enter your apartment every six months for an inspection."

"Okay."

"Okay?"

"Okay, I won't tell you."

Jacquard went silent but his body language was screaming.

"Jac, you're scaring me. Are you saying that they weren't sent by the manager?"

"No, what I'm saying is that you needed to check every time and in light of what happened today, it is always a possibility. Is it in your lease that they will send someone out?"

Now Charlotte was the one quiet.

"Charlotte Hope, did you even sign a lease?"

"Oh, I did. I just haven't looked at it since I signed it." She ended her statement with a sheepish grin.

Jac rubbed the back of his neck. "Call Mark, tell him where to find it, and have him bring it back with him."

"I can't, really. I mean I can tell him where all my papers are, but that's as close as I can get."

Jac shook his head and his lips quivered, trying to suppress a smile. He couldn't get enough of this woman and now that she was his, things would change. She let everything else go except her work. It was cute and scary.

She picked up her phone.

"And Charlotte?"

"Hmm?" she answered absently.

"When we get this mess figured out, you and I are going to have a talk about the way you've been living your life."

"You mean the life I don't have that it seems everyone is interested in? Fine, just don't forget you like me the way I am when we have this talk."

"Oh, I'm going to carry that in the forefront of my mind, believe me."

As soon as they pulled into his designated spot in the office garage, Sharlee jumped out of the SUV, almost hitting Jac in the face with the door.

"Oh, I'm so sorry Jac. I didn't mean to do that. Did I hit..."

Her eyes grew large as he calmly stepped around the open door and into her space, crowding her far past her normal comfort zone, but this was Jac. She didn't have a bubble where he was concerned. When this man got closer, her libido heated and her sex dampened.

"I think we'll be having a talk sooner rather than later, sweetheart. Gather what you need for the day and leave the rest. We have a lot to do, but you need to understand that things are different now and one of those things is that my woman does not open her own door unless she's driving."

"Jac that's nice but unnecessary. I like to be my own person, you know that."

"And I like to treat a lady like she is one. Besides, it's important that I have control of the environment before you exit the car. So when with me, and unless impossible, you wait until I open the door."

She turned and shut the door. "I still say it's unnecessary. No one else makes me do that, well, except for Monroe. And Garrett. The rest respect my right to be my own woman. You could learn from—"

The sound that echoed in the underground space was loud. The cause left an explosion of sting as he calmly laid another smack on her butt. Even in this awkward position, it hurt much more than she'd have expected with sweats on.

"What the fucking hell!" A large hand clamped her lips closed.

"You need to bring it down, baby. You're upset and I get it but that mouth of yours is writing checks your bottom won't want to pay." He kissed her quickly before placing his hand on the small of her back and guiding her to the elevator. "The women in my life, whoever they are, do not curse like a Marine recruit. Ever."

"What women?"

"Past, baby. You are my woman now. There won't ever be any others."

"Never?"

"Nope, never. Now, back to the language."

"You say things like Charlie Foxtrot all the time."

"And so can you. I say it like that so others aren't offended." The elevator doors closed, and he pulled her into his embrace, kissing the top of her head. "I get that things are confusing, but I promise it will settle down again. Just know that while the dynamic for us, and in some ways in the office, will be changing, the basics will stay the same."

"Right. Does that mean that I'm supposed to give over to you in everything?"

"Not at all. I don't want a woman who is dependent on me to get through her day, but I do want to be the man in our relationship."

Charlotte nodded. "The boss. Being in your arms makes me believe you'll take care of everything, but I'm a grown up. I can get through this mess, but I'd prefer to do it with you." She sighed. "I just want this day to end. It's like I've stepped into an alternate universe."

"Me too, but I'm going to take care of everything. Not alone, so don't get irritable, but you aren't doing any of it alone, either. We're a team." He leaned down to place a final kiss on Sharlee's lips before the elevator doors slid open. "For many reasons, for a while, you're going to find this easier and harder. Then you won't know how you survived." The door opened. "I'll get you another cup of coffee," Jac said, "because you're going to be busy pulling video and going through all the recordings of your apartment that we have. Check with Kaden and while he gets a little shut eye, you can start looking for who was in the apartment besides us. I know it's Saturday, but I don't have your equipment set up at my place, so we have to work here."

"Got it. Do we have to do it legally?"

"Don't ask, just get it done."

Chapter 15

E leven hours later, Jac turned his office light off, locked the door and turned in the direction of Sharlee's office. "It's late. Time we close up shop and go home. We'll have things transferred this week so you can work at the house when needed."

"What?" She yawned. "Oh, is it that late? I feel like I've been down so many rabbit trails, I hop now." She looked at the time. "Wow that is late. I guess I missed lunch and almost dinner too. Probably why I'm hungry, huh?" She wiggled her shoulders. "All I remember is the guys coming and going. Did someone bring my car?"

"Yes, but I'm not letting you drive it tonight. You're too tired."

"Ridiculous, besides, you're tired too."

"Yes, too tired to argue so get your things and come on. We need to make sure you don't miss lunch again. We'll pick up something for dinner on the way."

"Jac, I can cook."

"That's a relief." He smiled.

She shook her head and smiled back. She couldn't believe how nervous she was. No, take that back, she was on the petrified side.

"Cute. But I would enjoy not doing it tonight. Thanks."

He leaned down to kiss her. "You're welcome."

Sharlee watched Jac glance over at her as they stopped at the gate, grabbed the food delivered just moments before, leaving the gate guards their portion. Then he drove to the circular drive in the front of his house and veered to the right where his garage was. This was definitely a country estate.

She had been there a few times for gatherings with the staff or team. It was an impressive, two-story home with many rooms. He said he got it for a steal, but Sharlee knew that even at a bargain, it was expensive.

"This house has always impressed me. You must have paid a fortune."

"Actually, this was my parents' home, and I bought it from them. So I got the best deal."

He smiled and her nether regions wiggled and grew wet. The grounds were simple but lovely and the stable was well equipped. His horses were his pride and joy. She was overwhelmed to live in a place where there was a five-car garage, and an indoor pool and stables.

"Let's get you inside. I'll grab the bags if you'll carry the dinner."

After handing Charlotte her computer bag and the food, he grabbed the rest of the luggage and lead the way into the house.

Sharlee had expected Jac to lay out the rules and all that he intimated in the car that morning, but he made no move to do that. She must have looked exhausted. They turned on a movie after dinner and Jac slowly massaged her everywhere he could reach from his position. The next thing she knew, she was waking up to a warm body next to hers.

Startled, she inched away until she inhaled that undeniable scent of Jac. He pulled her closer to him and tucked his body around hers before kissing the side of her neck. She snuggled in and fell back to sleep. The next time she woke up, it was to a wet tongue on her nipple and then a mouth sucking her breast inside its warm moistness.

Sharlee moaned. "Mmm, I haven't been woken up like that ever. I could get used to it."

Lifting his head and letting go of the breast he was lavishing his attentions on for a moment, Jac grinned. "Good, because it's going to be the preferred way you wake up from now on."

"No arguments there." She grew quiet. The newness was still scary. "Jac, um, I need to tell you I don't have much experience." He stopped and gazed at her.

"You've not got much experience in what, exactly?"

"I mean, I do have, uh experience, but..." She shrugged. Her face was hot from her embarrassment.

Jac smiled. "I like it that way. Sweetheart, that's a gift."

He lowered his head and attached his lips and tongue to the sister breast. Streaks of fire shot to her sex as though there was a direct line from her tingling breasts to her throbbing clit. The deep tingling ran throughout her pussy, like a burst of sensation, hot and sizzling once it reached the farthest point of her nerve endings. She moaned.

He lifted his head slightly. In an instant, the worry that had flourished in her mind for a long time resurfaced. She was so inexperienced and a man like Jacquard Reynaud could probably write the book on how to please a woman whereas Sharlee had never had anything but vanilla sex.

"Baby, what's wrong? What are you thinking about so hard?" His hand stroked her inner thigh sending streaks of desire throughout her body.

"It's just that, the only sex I've ever had has been basic sex in the extreme." Somehow, she knew that Jac was anything but strictly vanilla because he'd already spent more time waking her up this morning than the whole sex act had taken in her two previous encounters.

Hot air and a gravelly whisper fell across her ear. "Okay, so you know the basics." He smiled. "I said I like it that way."

"No." She looked in his handsome face and then down to her hands.

"What's wrong, sweetheart? What are you thinking about? Worrying about?"

She shook her head because she couldn't get the words out. She also knew she risked Jac thinking she wasn't attracted to him because she didn't reciprocate. It wasn't that she didn't want to she just didn't know how. He had no idea that her little experience equaled nearly none.

"Charlotte?"

"Um, I'm good."

"Do you need a spanking?"

"No, why would you ask me that?" She turned in his direction as she spoke, her face in a deep frown.

"I ask because you just lied to me. I know we haven't had time to discuss expectations, but you already know lying won't be tolerated. So I ask again, what's wrong?" His expression hardened.

She fluttered her hand in the air. "Fine, I don't have much experience. In fact, I have almost no experience. Shocking given my age, I know, but it's true. I don't want to let you down, but I don't even know how not to disappoint you."

"Come here." Rearranging his body, he pulled her on top of him to lie between his legs, her head coming to rest on his chest. He ran his fingers though her hair, kissing the top of her head as his hand made its way down her back in soothing strokes.

"I mean, twice. I've had sex twice. Neither one of them spent any time in foreplay. At. All."

"Listen baby. I'm older than you are by about eight years. I've had my share of lovers over the years. I don't expect you to compete with me in that way and I'm damn glad you haven't had much experience. I know it's chauvinistic of me to want you to be newer at this part of our relationship, but there it is. I like to know I'm the first one to do things with you."

"Well, I'm no virgin but I've heard some guys don't want to have sex with someone who can't satisfy them."

Her muffled words spoken against his chest sent moist heat over his nipple, she slipped her tongue out and swiped it lightly and he shivered at the eroticism of it.

"Did you feel me tremble?"

"Yes, are you cold?"

"No, aroused. That little breath over my nipple did it. Then your tongue caressed my nipple. You arouse me by being in my room, on my mind, in my dreams. My cock is granite right now." He took her hand and placed it over the hardening in his shorts. "See? That's all you, sweetheart. And the men who want experience are lazy. A real man, one who cares about you, will take whatever you bring him and cherish it. He will want to show you a love that you make together, share with each other, and a relationship that you build as you grow in time."

"I like that idea." She hugged him.

"Good. Now, we'll talk plenty later on, but here's the thing. I want to learn what you like, to make every part of our life enjoyable. You'll learn what I like. We'll do this as one because no matter how much or little we know about the mechanics of love or being with another person, we're new and what we have is new. This morning, just let me love you. My job is to bring you enjoyment without expecting you to do anything in return. You're responsible for nothing, understand?"

"But it seems so unfair."

"I'll be fine because before we're done here, I'm going to sink into that delectable pink confection you are housing between those fine thighs of yours. Let me learn you?"

She nodded. "Okay."

"One last thing you need to know up front. In this room or during lovemaking, I'm the leader. There will be times that I defer to you at work and home and the same for you, but in here, like this, I direct our play. You stiffened again. You'll understand that it isn't like it sounds. You'll be so satisfied you won't want it any other way. Just go with me on this for now, yeah?"

She nodded again. "Yeah. For now."

"That's my girl. Now roll over and lay back, I need to start my loving all over again."

Jac lay against her side after she was flat on her back, throwing his leg over hers. It was heavy. She never thought about what they meant that muscle was heavier than fat, but this was the example. His body seemed to fit perfectly against hers. She moaned her arousal as he kissed her cheek, moving down her jawline to her slender neck. Kissing, sucking to almost pain and then licking. The tingles caused her to wiggle, her breathing hitched. Her belly was aching with a peculiar feeling.

She'd experienced lust before and she'd masturbated plenty of times to the mental image of Jac, but this was different. More powerful, wilder than her little made-up scenarios. Her nipples hurt, they were so hard, and miraculously, they continued to tighten. The discomfort was kissed away by Jac, suckled and nipped until she released little musical notes of yearning. The pain was morphing into shallow breaths, and a slippery sex.

Jac kissed her tummy, and the muscles tightened. He tongued her belly button. He continued downward. Oh no, he wouldn't do that, would he? What if she had sweated in the night? Her musky scent would put him off. She might stink. Her hands flew down to cover her wetness, stopping him from going further. The slap on her hands vibrated into her pussy.

"Arms at your sides," was all he said.

She obeyed, but she quickly had them over her muff again, pushing him away when he approached again. "You don't have to... I don't expect you to... do... ah, *that*."

He pushed her hands away and quickly rubbed his face in her muff. Then bit her labia, first one lower lip, then the other. It stung, almost hurt. She wiggled her discomfort. "Ow."

"I want to love you, but I'll punish you if you stop me from doing what I want to do. If I'm actually hurting you, say so. If something is wrong, tell me. But if you are just uncomfortable or think I'm doing something I don't want to do, then you say nothing. I'm going to push you further each time, not to scare you or hurt you, but to allow you to explore your sexuality. Now, hands over your head, hold the headboard if you need to but do not put your hands down again. If you disobey me, I'm going to punish you."

He meant it. Jac nodded at her to encourage her compliance.

Slowly, she raised her hands until they were over her head and then his stiffened tongue slid past her puffy lower lips and down the center of her wet channel. Her fingers curled around the spindles in the headboard. Every muscle in her body clenched. Her hands flew to his head. He lifted up and moved slightly. The sting was unbelievable and yet she thought she might just climax from that slap on her sex. It hurt, and it lit sparklers all inside. Fluid gushed.

"I told you where to put those hands. Looks like you get spanked on your pretty pussy for naughtiness." Three swats brought on an orgasm that slammed into Sharlee and took over her entire body.

Nothing penetrated her mind but sensation.

"You like that, I see. I'll note that for the next time you need punishment. I'm coming in baby. You're sopping wet so I know you're ready. Don't worry, I'll go slow and easy."

Sharlee hardly knew what he was saying as she scrambled to think clearly again. She watched him rise up over her and following the contours of his flexed stomach, she found the arrow of hair pointing the way to his engorged cock. Large, purple, and straining, she could just make out the fluid leaking from its tip. Her hand touched the mushroom shaped head and the sound he made was full of angst. She nearly yanked her hand back. Instead she stopped massaging him.

"Touch me. It's okay. You just felt so good, baby. The hurt is a good kind of ache."

She wrapped her fingers around his stalk and caressed the skin, exploring, and then she touched his deeply wrinkled sac, scrunched up tight to his body. Men's bodies were not unfamiliar to Charlotte, but this was the first one she had ever cared about enough to get the loving right.

Jac spoke through gritted teeth. "Sorry baby, but you have to let me visit now. I'll let you explore again but right now, I need inside. I won't last long this time."

He slid inside slowly. Painstakingly slow. His moans of ecstasy were gratification enough to give her the courage she needed to relax in the invasion. So tight. Encouraged and emboldened, Sharlee met him the last little bit by raising her hips.

"Don't move, baby. I have to get my bearings again. I have to gain some control or it will be all over in two seconds."

Sharlee loved that she'd taken his self-control and played havoc with it. She had power too, it seemed. Jac's rhythmic movements began and soon they were both breathing in shallow, labored gasps. The slick, smooth pistoning was slow and steady at first. Then the momentum steadily increased until he was pounding inside and she couldn't believe what she had been missing but glad she'd waited for this man. He leaned further over her, rubbing her clit, but she didn't need any additional help. His cock touched a spot she didn't know existed, and she was suddenly crying out in fulfillment, she fell over the precipice of the wonder that making love with Jac was.

His sounds of release kept her in the throes of orgasm for longer. Finally spent, they fell back to sleep for another hour. It was Sunday. Charlotte wondered if they could do this every day, going in late to the office. It was good to be dating the boss. It came with some definite advantages.

Often, Sharlee thought of the beauty of evening sex with Jac as the days were long. The team trickled in and out of the building working their contracts in an almost never-ending stream of briefings, research, gearing up, heading out, checking in, repeat. Sharlee stayed in the office like a pampered princess with irritated, hypervigilant keepers.

But between other work, she and Kaden finally came to the end of the exhaustive search, with no solid answers. She had traced part of the information stream to enough dead ends to tangle the world. Finally, after she had traced the last link to an innocuous office in the government and she meant paper pushers only, she called it done.

"Sorry guys but I just can't crack this one. The worry is that if I can't trace them back to an original source and the sources I do reach are non-entities, then they have found someone better than I am to do the work. Not to be tooting my own horn, but I'm pretty damn good. I know a few that are better, but they aren't always working for the home team. Well one is but the rest go with the money, usually. Ethical motivation isn't their reasoning behind taking a job."

"Get me the list, Sharlee. I'll do my own investigative work."

"Okay. But it still means we're no closer to who was tracking me than before. And if the people on this list are cyber smoke, how are you going to find them and decide if they are part of the problem or not?"

"By association."

"In cyberspace."

"Not true," said Monroe. "We know our person is likely on your list or associated with someone on your list. Then we know that they have on the ground associates. It is likely that our guy isn't one of your cyber buddies but one of our Feds associated with Kyle's case or what Kyle was doing. An administrator or something. That narrows things."

"He's right. Garrett, you and Monroe divide and conquer but it will have to be secondary to our open contracts." Both men nodded at Jac's instructions. Jac added. "Charlotte, until we know the whole story you don't go anywhere alone, understood?"

"Wait, you can't make me do that. I have my freedoms just like all Americans."

Jac continued without addressing her flippant statement. "And take a copy of your list and run as deep a check on each as you are able. Look to see if there are any connections. That will help. The guys can play the human connections, but you have the cyber links. Are any of your guys connected to any of our connections."

"Jac, you can't make me a prisoner over this. What if we never find the *him* that Kyle was talking about? We don't even know if that is who was following me or spying on me."

"We'll cross that bridge when we come to it."

Garrett asked, "Could it be connected to your outside contracts?"

"I told you to get rid of those. You won't listen. Now it's a safety issue." Jac's voice was hard. "Complete these two you have now, and don't accept another."

"Stop and listen to yourself. I was asked if the cameras could've been placed by one of my contract holders. Since they are all for one government entity or another, I am very careful. But it was a suggestion of possibility, Jac, not a statement of fact. I've been doing my private contracts for years without incident."

"That you know of."

"Without incident."

Ignoring Sharlee, Jac continued. "Okay guys, do what you can with the list she gives you." It was an obvious dismissal. Sharlee scraped her chair loudly as she stood. He turned in her direction. "Not you. I've a few things left to say to you."

"I bet you do, but I have a job, no several, that I need to get back to."

Jac rose, blocking off the exit after the two men left. He closed the door. "Sit down."

Chapter 16

"Jac, I'm going to work on the list. Please move."

"No. Sit down."

She tried to go around him to reach the door, but he leaned back on it. She walked farther into the room then turned to face him, hands clenched. "Dammit, you're not my keeper just because you're my lover."

"Oh, sweetheart, you have so much to learn. Sit down. Now." He advanced on her position in the room.

"Now, Jac, this isn't fair. I'm a grown woman and I can handle my job and my life without you making and changing my decisions."

He reached his hand up to her face and smiled when he saw she didn't flinch. She wasn't afraid of him, good. He never wanted her fear, but only occasional obedience would never do. He saw her suck her lip between her teeth in a nervous response. His thumb pulled her lip out and he captured it with his own lips. The kiss began tenderly, but quickly grew into something needy and urgent. It gratified him when she responded greedily. Jac drew back as he ended the kiss. She whimpered.

He retraced his steps, reached back and locked the door before leading her to the desk. Leaning down, he hit the privacy windows. She knew what was coming if he didn't get his way or wasn't satisfied. She was annoyed and aroused, which only proved to irritate her more. He sat in his chair and opened his arm in invitation. She accepted, almost leaping onto his lap. He pulled her close and kissed the top of her head. After a moment of cuddling, he straightened them both.

"Now listen first, then talk. I'm your boss here, and I know this dual affiliation is in its infancy, but I don't intend to remind you of my position or yours again and again. You don't argue like that with me in front of anyone. You have always been respectful, and I require you to continue to be so now. If this were anyone else's apartment that these things happened in, I would start the buddy system. I'm your buddy when you're not here." His tone deepened. "You will follow my orders on this because I'm your boss. You'll do it willingly because you know you are important to me. If you find neither of those reasons are enough, I'll place you under house arrest until I figure this out. And since it appears as though it might take some time to untangle, I wouldn't recommend that alternative."

"Jac, come on, I'll be fine. No one's tried to hurt me."

"And no one will if I can help it. Now we have things to do, and we can discuss this again later tonight. Until we do, you stay inside."

"Fine."

He leaned over and kissed her hard and fast. "You're getting a spanking tonight."

"You can't, um, do that, just because I disagree with you."

He barked a laugh. "Are you sure?"

"Well, you shouldn't."

"I'll be the judge of that. I think you need to relieve some of the stress."

"Not hard."

"And now you're topping from the bottom, like trying to drive from the back seat, not done without consequences."

"But I might have a good idea."

"You're stalling." He pushed her out of his lap. "Get out of here and get back to work, brat." Jack kissed her nose and swatted her butt before she smiled teasingly at him, unlocked the door, and walked out.

Handing the list to Garrett and Monroe, Sharlee looked around and noticed that no one else was in the office. Support had another set of offices at the end of the hall. They stationed Becky and reception near the entrance at the elevators.

Now's my chance, a quick in and out will get me what I need without all these prying eyes.

She popped her keys, a credit card and her license into her back pocket, then slid her phone in her front pocket, pulling her shirt over the top of her jeans. Turning toward the bathroom, she quietly slipped into the stairwell next to the ladies'. Exiting she took the elevator on the floor below, grabbing a taxi from the line of them that were ever present outside the busy executive building.

Jumping inside the cab, she rattled off the address to her apartment and soon they were pulling up into the front drive of her building. Her heart was pounding, and her breath was quick and shallow. Her phone was ringing by the time she jumped out onto the pavement. She glanced at the phone display. Jacquard, just as she expected.

"Hi Jac. I had to step out for a moment, but I'll be back shortly. I'm getting some lunch. Do you want anything?"

"Dammit, Charlotte Hope, I want you to bring your sassy ass back here immediately and present it for discipline. What the hell do you think you're doing? Didn't you hear anything I said to you earlier? Are you begging for a spanking because if that's it, you just have to ask. You need to know that."

"No, I'm picking up a few things and grabbing lunch. Jac, I have to go. I'll be back soon, promise." Sharlee hung up before he could respond further. She'd heard him. She knew he was worried, but she was a big girl.

A relationship with Jacquard meant so much more than her other dates or boyfriends. It was freeing, intense, full of accountability, and it wasn't lonely. She didn't miss being lonely at all. In his hands were love, fun, security, and something else. When he swatted her butt for accountability or warning, or stress, hers or his, it made their bond stronger, more secure. Just as his teaching her all the ways he knew to satisfy each other in areas outside of sex was careful and thorough.

Sharlee wanted more, but he'd only go at the pace he set and no amount of begging seemed to change his mind, well, usually. She explored more adventuresome sex with him and indulged in long sensual scenes of lovemaking and in that area, he was the master. Her sexual prowess had been minimal, instinct only, but he had been coaxing her into new areas of gratification that she now craved. Jac knew what she needed, somehow he just knew. But she needed more than sex, she needed her autonomy.

Her phone rang again as she stepped off the elevator onto the correct floor for her apartment. She ignored the call. Now that she knew about them, she checked around and found the small camera and a little red light. She took her phone out and took a picture of the camera instead of answering the call. It was Jac anyway.

Taking out her keys, Charlotte first turned the handle out of habit and was surprised that it twisted. She slowly opened the door to her apartment and was shocked at the total chaos in front of her. She'd never been a great housekeeper, but this was way beyond messy. You'd think the guys would have been better with her things.

Pocketing her keys, she heard something rattle in the bedroom. Her heart pounded heavily, and her head seemed to tighten in apprehension. She held her breath. Tummy rolling, she grabbed the baseball bat from the hall closet. Her granddad had insisted years ago that she own it for safety. She'd never had to lift it in self-defense before now.

She didn't have her gun. Jac held it in his gun safe. She would have to do with the bat. Did she call out or just walk in further? Her chest hurt with the pounding of her heart. Her breath was labored and keeping it silent was almost impossible. There was another movement.

Her fear was beginning to take over. This could be real trouble. Jac would kill her if she got hurt, but these were her things in this apartment. Gathering all the courage she could muster, she raised the bat and walked stealthily toward her bedroom.

She tripped over debris on the floor and fumbled the bat as she tried to grab the hall closet door frame to stabilize without much success. Frightened, all semblance of misplaced bravado gone, Sharlee backed up trying not to stumble as she reached the doorway. Then she was out of the apartment. Unfortunately, she wasn't the only one exiting.

Before she could register it as more than a moving blob barreling towards her, she was hit hard in the chest, knocking the air from her lungs. Her body flew against the outer hall wall, her head bouncing as it hit. Another person was right behind the first and Sharlee desperately tried to refill her lungs as she threw her bat at the moving person, tripping but not slowing him.

A door opened and then closed further down the hall. She turned to look but saw nothing. No help from the neighbors, then. Sharlee slid her body down the wall and pulled her phone out of her pocket. Her chest and head hurt. She was too dizzy to find Jac's number. Panic was setting in. She'd not experienced one in several years. Not since she landed the job at Jacquard and Associates.

She used the verbal command mode. "Call Jac," she rasped.

"Sharlee, where the hell are you?"

"Jac." The quality of her voice was enough conversation for him.

His tone softened to a caress. "Where are you, baby?"

"My apartment."

"On my way." His next words were kind of jumpy like he was moving fast as he spoke, and she had no doubt that he was. "Are you hurt? Do you need an ambulance?"

"I'm hurting but not harmed and not ambulance worthy." Her breaths were shallow by necessity. It hurt. "I'm trying to stop my panic."

"I'll bring Monroe. Are you safe?"

"Yes, I think so. Just hurry."

"You're safe. You're secure. There is nothing to harm you. Jac is coming. Hold on. You're safe." She closed her eyes to concentrate on the words and thoughts, but did she pass out, because it seemed like she had just disconnected the call and Jac was right there.

"Wow," she said with effort, "you were quick."

"Charlotte, listen to me sweetheart. Are you good to sit here? We need to clear the place."

"They're gone."

Monroe and Jac verified she was right and came back to attend to her. Once they were sure there were no broken or dislocated bones, Jac helped her up and swung her into his arms. Her eyes grew large.

"Gonna puke." He stood her on her feet but held on tight, taking her weight while she did more gagging than anything.

"Right, its acute care for you and if you utter one word of complaint, it's the emergency room."

"Okay, I don't feel very well, anyway."

He nodded his satisfaction and spoke with Monroe before scooping Charlotte into his arms again and strode toward the elevator.

"There's a camera right there, too," she said while snuggled into his chest. His grunt was comforting. Jac would take care of everything.

Things seemed to jump into high gear after Charlotte had gone to the apartment, but she was happy with some of their accomplishments. She ended her lease at Jac's insistence and moved into his home permanently. She was hesitant to do it but more hesitant to stay in the apartment another year and with the lease conveniently ending, she could make the transition.

Sharlee just wished Jac would quit going on about the same things. Like her outside work. She kept a few private contracts that annoyed Jac often, but he didn't push it, just grunted and had sex more often. Sharlee could handle that.

She decided that the reason she kept them was mostly for her independence. She wanted to be her own woman. Jacquard Reynaud wanted her to be as independent as she could, but he obviously didn't know how to allow that. This helped them both in some small way.

The cameras were all retrieved, including the new one that had been replaced at the elevator. It was evident that several new ones were strategically located but not hidden well enough. Once Carter and Kaden had them all in their hands, the trace had begun on who used these rather exclusive models. The government for one.

Jac had Charlotte work on finding out what her last clients used. She found some of them used none, which sounded un-believable. Several entities used the model found in the hall-way. She wanted to approach them on it, but the team said it was too dangerous right now.

Jac had gotten serious then. Jac's need to know where Sharlee was at all times bordered obsessive. Unfortunately, with Sharlee, when Jac's back was against the wall, he became a wolverine in protective mode. Charlotte wasn't very receptive to that Jac. The conference room had gone quiet.

"You finish these contracts and then you don't take on more. If they aren't contracts that I or the team has vetted, then you don't work them. Do I make myself clear?"

"You can't make me stop, Jac. I can do outside contracts be-cause it is in our contract."

"I'm rewriting our contract."

"I won't sign it."

"Are you kidding me? One or more of your contracts has been spying on you, following you, rifling through your stuff. If you won't protect yourself, then I'm doing it for you. If you want to keep your job here, then you will cease accepting outside contracts."

"Great. I'm done here."

She slammed out of the conference room. Jac knew he'd gone too far, but he didn't know any other way to force her to keep safe.

"Dammit Jacquard, what the hell did you do that for? If she quits, I mean really quits, I'm going to dip your balls in boiling oil." Garrett looked at Kaden. "You have the golden tongue. Go after her and try to smooth some of this over. Use logic and understanding. You know how to do it better than the rest of us."

"What about Becky?"

"She is dealing with family issues right now so you're up," said Carter.

Jac decided not to ask how Carter knew about Jac's personal assistant's private life. He wasn't sure he wanted that answer right now. Garrett followed Kaden out of the conference room in disgust. Carter and Mark left to resume their jobs mumbling their discontent while Monroe sat at the table.

"Go ahead and do your worst, then leave me alone. I had to push her to decide because I can't deal with this any longer. I love her, man. It would kill me if something happened to her because I didn't tell her the potential danger she was in. I had to prepare her. I need her to let me take protective measures."

"For the sake of this conversation, say I agree that she needed to know about the danger around her and I do. I think she's a super intelligent woman who can easily run circles around any one of us in her area of expertise. She is vulnerable because she trusts too easily but it is also why she fits so well with us. Sharlee trusted us without fanfare. She got to know us, we dealt fairly with her, and that earned her undying trust. But giving a woman like that an ultimatum will bite you in the ass every time."

Jac hated when Kaden and Carter talked about strategies of how to deal with their women and each had one that usually lasted a couple of months. Mark didn't even do more than date in rotation because he didn't commit and Garrett's woman of over a year just walked out last month. He was hurting more than he'd admit. Monroe hooked up and seemed happy to keep it that way. Until Charlotte walked into their lives, Jac was too.

He ran his hand through his hair and sighed. "Okay, so what do I do? How do I fix this?"

Garrett answered from the door. "You go find her and then tell her you were wrong. You explain you're worried she's in danger, but you'll protect her with all you have. *We* will protect her. Tell her she means something to you, personally, not as an employee or team member but Charlotte is important to Jacquard. And then you beg, man, because we need her on the team, and you need her in your life." No one said that it sounded like Garrett was talking through his own pain from experience, but they knew.

"Thanks and if you mention this touchy-feely conversation I'll deny it, then I'll cut off your junk and leave it for the buzzards, both of you."

Jac left with Garrett and Monroe laughing after him.

Chapter 17

Sharlee was through talking for a while. She'd tried to understand why Jac was so demanding and all she could come up with was that he was used to being the boss. Then Kaden had run her down and helped her see things differently. Yes, Jacquard Reynaud had been the leader in whatever he did in the military for over fifteen years. The army had seen his leadership qualities early on and groomed him for their needs and then he had been assigned to a multi-service task team.

After a few years he took over leadership of this rather covert group and that was all Kaden would say except that it was where they all had met and learned to respect Jac and his decisions.

"Except when it comes to you. You are his weakness," said Kaden.

Sharlee wasn't sure that was good or bad, but she could talk to Kaden and needed to talk since she had no longtime girlfriend and no sisters. She had become better friends with Jac's personal assistant Becky, and she'd recently met Jessie, the fairly new accountant for the group. She was fun, but Sharlee didn't want to talk about their boss to them. Odd but it didn't seem to matter with Kaden.

"What do you mean, exactly?"

"I mean he cares about you. He is crazy about you, actually. We all have girlfriends or hook up and date but when you came on scene Jac quit."

"Quit dating?"

"Quit everything. He is careful to watch that you are taken care of, we all are, but for Jac, it is an obsession. It's part of his day to make sure you are cared for and that your needs are met."

"Oh. I know he likes me; I mean, he says he does and I'm here with him but..."

"Jac has only had a couple of exclusive girlfriends for as long as I've known him and that has been over ten years. The military was his live-in lover. He's never had another until you. When he retired and left a blanket invitation for those who wanted an outside job to call him, I did it when I was medically retired because he has integrity. He doesn't say or do what he doesn't mean or believe in. He wants you because you mean something big to him."

"I wondered why you were here, but not old enough for retirement. I did wonder how he could engender such loyalty. I get it from my perspective, but now, I get it from yours, too."

"Yeah, my elbow was nearly shattered and after I recovered, and they replaced it, they'd have allowed me back to soldier but not on the team. I decided it was the team or nothing so I called Jac and had a job the next day." Kaden put his forearms on his thighs and leaned forward. "All I'm saying is if Jac has a blind spot in his judgement, it's you. You're going to have to decide if you can handle that and the occasional bad reaction he has with you or if you can't. Does he mean enough to you to figure the rest out? I recommend deciding now because it will make life so much easier for all of us, you and Jac most especial-ly."

Charlotte stayed quiet for a while as Kaden talked about a variety of things. Sharlee knew he was giving her time to process. But did she need it or want it? Could she handle Jac not taking her opinions into consideration when he had a different idea? She wasn't his recruit or trainee and while it was still his team, she didn't have to stay if he wouldn't respect her input enough to at least listen and consider it.

No, she couldn't stay if he didn't figure out how to treat her as an equal member of the team both in the office and at home. They either showed mutual respect or it wouldn't work.

JAC DIDN'T KNOW WHERE to look for Sharlee, but he did know how to track and triangulate a cell phone signal be-cause she had shown him. Garrett was right. Sharlee was smart, talented, and running scared. Jac rolled his eyes. The little minx was so smart she had turned her phone off. Where would she go? The lake, she loved the lake. With his car pointed in that direction, he was well on his way when he received a call from Kaden.

"Kaden, where are you? Did you find Charlotte?" Jac pulled his car over after listening to his friend as he explained where they were and what was going on. "I understand and I'm on my way. Hey, thanks."

Pulling up into his driveway, Jac closed the electronic inner gate, driving to the garage and sat for a few moments. He need-ed to go slow and not mess this up. He loved she came home to his, and now her, place when she needed to find comfort, but he hated she was taking it from someone else. Jac looked up when the back door closed. Kaden walked to the car and waited until Jac got out of the car.

"She's upset and afraid that you're angry with her. Actually, she's positive you're going to ask her to leave. I couldn't convince her otherwise. She needs reassurance and you're the only one who can give it to her. Don't mess this up because I need her on the team."

"I've already heard this from Monroe and Garrett. I get it. I screwed up."

"Then you better get her to understand that and then listen to her. She isn't spouting off some garbage, she makes sense."

"Thanks, man. Goodnight."

"Night, boss."

Jac reached the door and drew a deep breath in, then blew it out in determination. As he entered the house, he forgot that he had no idea where she was. He listened and followed the sound of what he soon identified as his gym equipment. He walked in the room and stood behind his girl walking on the treadmill. He stripped to his shorts. Stepping up to the universal, he began doing repetitions.

His Charlotte hated exercise and if she was here burning off energy, then she'd been angry and hurt. He was going to wait her out. Either she'd stop when she saw him or ignore him until she was spent. Then they'd talk. Jac had been here many times when he was too wound up to be productive. He'd get rid of some of his extra energy too as he waited for her to be ready to talk this out. He could and would give her the floor until she yielded it, if ever.

KADEN LEFT AND WITHIN moments, she heard another sound and knew without looking that it was the man she dreamed about and craved. Jac had found her, and she smiled when she imagined what he was thinking. She was walking on the treadmill, the woman who didn't exercise except the minimum needed to stay minimally fit.

The sound changed, but he made no move to speak to her. Jac was a rather impatient man when things weren't going his way. He'd climbed on his universal machine and had begun repetitions. She loved to watch his muscles ripple. He wasn't yet forty and his sweaty well-defined body would create cream in hers every time.

She surreptitiously cut her eyes in the direction of the sound and saw him staring at her, working his body. His cock was at half-mast. How, she had no idea, but he was aroused even when he was exercising. He didn't falter in his movements but continued to keep his eyes on her. She looked away and then back again. God she wanted him, cared about him. How was she going to tell him what she needed while he rocked her boat so completely?

Her step hesitated and then she stumbled as she tried to regain control. The machine shut down and his hand was on her, stabilizing her. Sharlee looked up into his eyes and there was a whole conversation there. He wanted her, cared for her, hoped they could work it out—all displayed in those eyes. There was also the protectiveness, a fierceness of ownership, a hint of control that he could never leave behind completely. This was Jac, her man. The one she'd have to leave if things didn't change enough. And it would kill her.

"Need a towel, sweetheart?"

"Yes."

He produced one out of seemingly thin air and stepped back to allow her to step down from the machine.

He nodded at the treadmill. "I was surprised. Did it help?"

Sharlee shrugged. "Yeah, well, I thought I would try it your way once. Still not a fan but it served a purpose."

She slowly walked toward the door and Jac followed, having retrieved a towel for himself. They headed toward the kitchen on the same floor. She pulled two bottles of water from the fridge and passed one to him. He reached over and twisted her top before accepting his bottle and uncapping it.

"Thanks."

His smooth throat column rippled as he drank half the bottle then finished it in two long drinks. He tossed it in the trash as he would when sinking a basketball. Like a normal moment in a normal life except theirs wasn't always normal.

Jac reached around her and asked as he opened a cupboard, "Hungry?"

"I could eat." She tentatively smiled.

"My specialty?"

"Take out?" Her laugh was mixed with a giggle.

He grinned back. "Brat. I meant steak and potatoes."

"Can we have corn on the cob? I know we have some frozen."

"Get it out," he said.

"And salad?"

He laughed. "Is my girl hungry?"

"Ravenous. All I had was a muffin this morning, and I worked out you know."

"Right, a full meal for my starving woman is coming right up."

The awkwardness was avoided. Charlotte was relieved. Jac was a big man with a big presence. They worked in companionable silence as they pulled the meal together. Sharlee knew there would still need to be what Carter called a "Come to Jesus" meeting but they could eat first.

The food smelled wonderful as it was cooking, and Sharlee was starving by the time Jac put her plate in front of her. There was nothing but the sound of satisfied and appreciative munching until they had slaked the first demands of hunger. Things slowed down then, and Sharlee took a break.

"I might have had an exaggerated understanding of how much I could eat."

"I'll always help you out, baby." He reached over and jabbed a bit of potato before popping it into his mouth with a smile. The message was a universal one. Problem solved.

"I wish we could settle all of our issues so easily," murmured Sharlee.

"Well, I think we can, but some issues require more thought."

"Maybe."

They finished dinner in relative silence, cleaned up, and loaded the dishwasher. They grabbed glasses of a sweet wine she had just discovered and Jac took Sharlee's hand, leading her into the living room. Setting their glasses down on the table, he sat first before pulling her onto his lap.

Jac kissed her cheek. "I know we need to talk but I don't want to do it so far apart."

"That's sneaky, Jac."

"Maybe, but I prefer to think of it as making things real. This is the real us, Sharlee. We're good together but the world keeps crowding in."

"So do you want me to talk first or do you want to?"

"I'd rather make love, but I guess this has to happen first."

She playfully punched his gut. "Jac, this is important. Okay, I'll go first." Jack sat quietly as Sharlee discussed her feelings.

"I have opinions and expertise Jac, and they are worth taking into consideration. I want to feel like I'm a real part of the team, not a princess with some occasionally useful skill set." She sat up straight in his lap and tried to scoot off.

"I'm listening. You don't have to get off my lap to get my attention. I hear what you're saying."

"I don't know if we can do this, Jac. I don't know if you can allow me to make my own judgement calls when they are mine to make."

"I want to. Okay. Well look at it this way. I'm not used to having a woman on my team, I already told you that soon after you signed on and I meant it. You're part of the team, a full member. I just don't know how to handle that all the time. Factor in that I have some strong feelings for you, which means I take your happiness and safety very seriously. It makes things even harder when I am positive your safety is being compromised and you won't accept my protective measures for you."

Sharlee looked into his eyes. "I want to be treated like what I say has meaning."

"Charlotte honey, it does, and it always has. Sometimes you get angry because you don't get your way and then you do things to prove you don't have to follow my rules. On the job, they're my rules to follow but you can be respectful and question them. You can't openly defy them without consequences, though. Anyone on the teams that want to defy me openly, or Garrett or Monroe for that matter, will find there will be consequences. Here in our private life, you are an equal partner that has equal say. It's just that sometimes, if you don't get your way because I'm adamant on an issue, you do whatever you can to get around it. You and I both know that isn't working well."

"I think you have tactfully called me a brat."

"Really? Because I thought I was very clear. You are a brat. Sometimes you're a sassy, cute one and sometimes an annoying naughty one, but a brat most definitely. Nevertheless, I promise to treat you like a full member of the team but that means in the places where we have given you a pass, you don't get one anymore."

"What are you talking about?"

"When you take a job and do more than you are authorized to do such as an inside camera or tapping into feeds when we're done with the job because you think we didn't get all the intel."

"Oh."

"Yeah, oh. Do it again and I will nail your ass to the wall. And I promise it won't be in a playful sexy way."

"But Jac, on that job I was right. We missed something, and it was a good thing I didn't let go right away."

"And if you feel that strongly about it you present at the table with all of us and we decide if we agree. But if we say no in a group, the answer is no, not wait until no one's looking. Got me?"

"Yes, sir."

"Good. Now we need to talk about the cameras that were trained inside and outside that apartment. I have no doubt that one of the hall cameras was from one of your government jobs."

"Okay, I agree you're probably right, but I can't quit the jobs with them because they are my access in for other jobs."

"You'll find another way."

Sharlee shook her head. "It doesn't work like that. Some of my most helpful resources are the databases in the government. The best way to use them is through the front door. They're on the lookout for the back-door people and almost totally ignore front entry users."

"I don't want them knowing everything you do."

"They don't. They had to put up physical cameras to access me at all. And besides, they probably were making sure that I did nothing that jeopardized my work with them, like meeting up with the wrong people and stuff. They need to be sure their investment is safe. You want that, too. It allowed me to prove I wasn't doing anything with Kyle."

"Yeah, but I don't do it on the sly. I don't like that others do."

Sharlee's eyebrows shot into her hairline. "Do you want to rephrase that, sir? I believe you misspoke."

"You're right, I did the same thing, but I care about you. I don't want you to be vulnerable if I'm not there to protect you or at least one of the guys. I know you can handle most things yourself, but it's just me. I have to sleep at night."

She snuggled in. "Okay, I'll let you protect me so long as you don't stop me doing what I need to do."

"So long as what you need to do is not interfering with your immediate safety," added Jac.

"Deal."

He kissed the top of her head. "Anything else we need to discuss before I take my brat to bed?"

"Not a thing, boss."

Chapter 18

"She did what?" asked Jac in a dangerously, too calm voice. Kaden groaned. "She sent some information to her government contacts and told them she had found the camera. She then discussed the ownership of the camera. And finally she explained that if it happened again, she'd not only stop taking their contracts, but she'd also hire us to protect her after taking contracts they didn't want her to work."

"You heard all of this?"

"Every damn word and I have to say, she did one hell of a job explaining her expectations. I only tell you because I was worried about the fallout or if you got a call from someone."

"Thanks. I'll cover it from here." He kept his counsel until they were driving home.

"Charlotte, have you heard from your contractors lately?"

"Why?" She wiggled in her seat and looked out her side window.

"I thought you were finishing a contract any day now."

"Oh. I did, so I called them to finish it out."

"And?"

"And what? We discussed business and then we hung up."

"Did any of that business include the camera from your elevators in the apartment?"

"Maybe."

"Did the team discuss information about the cameras and agree on who we would discuss things with and who we wouldn't?"

"Probably. What's this about?"

"A certain phone call you had earlier today."

Sharlee was quietly rearranging her purse. "Tapping my phone lines now? Fine, I did, but he just admitted it and said they wanted to know about you as much as me. Guess you have caught their attention. So if I wasn't working for you, then they wouldn't have likely put up the camera."

"Honey, people have been watching me, the teams since we opened our doors for business. There's nothing new there. You breaking our agreement is something to discuss, though."

"Well, maybe discussing that me working for you makes me more of a target so, there's that."

"Or more protected."

"Maybe. Just let me cook dinner first because I'm starving. Before you ask, I skipped lunch by accident. I was so caught up in finishing the private contract and what I was doing on Mark's assignment, it was almost time to go home before I realized it."

"Okay, let's get you fed. We can stop and get dinner if that would make life easier."

"No, I want a shower too."

"All right but when dinner is over we're having a conversation." He dropped his voice because that always got the best results. "You didn't discuss things with me first and that is always going to be a problem."

Sharlee sighed. "I know but I saw the chance, and I had to take it. I can't always stop to drag you into a room to finish a conversation. At some point, you are going to have to trust me with my own information."

Jac sat in the living room and waited for Charlotte to make her appearance. They'd cleared away the nice dinner she'd made and now it was time to get down to business. Charlotte had been subdued for the first few days as she recovered from her apartment experience which also included a mild concussion. Then the blow up in the office occurred that was put to rest with a mutual understanding. Now it was the following Friday and time to clear the air between them. He looked up to see his beautiful, nearly naked woman enter the room hesitantly. She had on a nightshirt that covered her butt but barely and he knew from experience, she had nothing underneath. His heart beat faster and his cock signaled its awakening. He put his hand out to her, watching as she placed her smaller one in his. He drew her closer.

"You're so beautiful, sweetheart." She shrugged.

Jac watched her as she got closer. "And you're worried."

"Yes," she whispered.

He pulled her between his spread thighs. "Yes. Earlier this week, I know you thought it was no big deal taking off to the apartment alone, until it was. Until you ran into trouble. But I mean for you to know that on so many levels you were wrong to disobey my new standing order which means it wasn't up for interpretation.

"Charlotte," Jac reached for her other hand and pulled her onto his lap. "I love you. I've loved you for so long I almost can't remember what it was like without you in my life. I'm not looking for some declaration from you, but I want you to know how precious you are to me. When I say you can't go anywhere alone for now, I get scared when you do dangerous things like going against my orders. And it irritates me. Then it makes my hand itchy."

She released a muffled sob. He was getting through to her.

"Even after I told you my reasons for wanting to keep this information about the cameras to ourselves for a while longer, you took a picture of the camera and called your contractor."

"I didn't see that there would be any real harm. And I didn't just call him. I waited until I had finished his contract."

He put his finger under her chin and lifted her face towards his. "We discussed roles and expectations not only at work but for our personal life as well. I am positive you thought I would have a problem with you discussing the cameras. Or with you sneaking out like a rebellious teen to go to your apartment when I had been clear about not going anywhere alone."

"But Jac, on the phone today, my main contractor, Mr. Grundle, finally admitted his office placed the camera in the hall upstairs at the elevator. He said they put it there not so much to protect me from unsavories, but to see if they could capitalize on the new permanent employers I had." She shook her head. "I wonder what they would've done if I didn't take their next contract. Would they have removed the camera? Or what if I no longer worked for you?"

"I don't know honey, but you could have compromised your safety by telling Grundle what you knew or he might not have admitted to it. Then he could have tried to put a camera on you again, or worse."

"I don't know. He said they wouldn't put one in my private residence, but the apartment owners had agreed they could put one in the hallway thinking it was more security they wouldn't have to pay for. So Grundle didn't place the cameras in my apartment. The cameras inside were placed by someone else and so were the inspections. The government had no need. And it means that three entities were spying on me. I should have stayed in hiding."

"The government shouldn't have done it at all."

"Would you listen to yourself? You did it. Some unknown other person did it. You all violated my privacy. Big time."

"I did it out of concern for your safety. Do you think that some cog in the government wheelhouse would care about you? The error was that we didn't tell you. That was wrong of me. But I can't bear the thought of something happening to you and I absolutely refuse to lose you because you thought I was too protective and too restrictive, so you went against my orders."

"I don't like people taking over my decisions. At least we have the answers to a few questions, anyway."

His brows grew tall and pointed causing her to sigh. He hugged her tight and leaned down to kiss the top of her head. "Ready?"

"Do we have to?"

"No."

"No?" she sighed. "But I know this is who you are, who we are together, and I'm good with it."

Jack kissed her again, this time on the lips and helped her to settle over his knee.

"Put both hands on the floor and if you are having trouble keeping your hands off your rear end while I am addressing its owner, I can put you in a different position that will make that impossible but I'm positive you will not be happy with it. Understood?"

"Yes, I get it Jac, just get it over with."

He smacked her butt lightly. "Brat."

If he could see her face he knew he would see her eyes roll. He was positively bouncing with excitement. He slapped her fleshy bottom cheeks. He loved her sass but now wasn't the appropriate time to be a brat, except it worked for him.

"Are you sure you can afford to be mouthy with me in this position, sweetheart?"

He slapped her butt several times with concentration. She answered the slaps with squeals and wiggles. He spanked in earnest, using slow deliberate swats then changing them up to hard and fast smacks. He spoke in between swats and wails of complaints. Her wiggles had increased.

"Be still, naughty girl. When you do not follow rules for your safety, your ass is polished a shiny red." His hand came down again, and she made a mewling sound that was so damn cute he hesitated before continuing. "I'm going to get down to the real spanking now."

"What is this you've been doing then if not a spanking?" Her breath was coming faster.

"A real spanking, like you have needed for quite some time. It will calm you down, get the sass under control, and make me feel like I've gotten my point across on the disobedience. But equally important is that we both crave it."

His hand came down time after time and he watched as her bottom progressed from blush to flush to fiery red. He rubbed between swats now. Every inch of her ass was covered by his hand leaving behind a residual sizzling message. A punishment was meant to be hard and fast in his book, so he made sure this spanking was both punishment and sensual. He would have her tonight.

His throbbing dick was as hard as he could ever remember it becoming. This woman was all he wanted, and she was wet. He could see it every time she kicked her legs. He'd thought to hold those wildly waving appendages down but then he couldn't gauge if she was okay or if she was really in distress. Once he had laid several hard swats on her thighs and told her to show some control over her legs or he'd have to, she moderated her movements.

"Jac, please, I can't do this anymore." Her voice was heavy with tears.

He stopped again and rubbed, grinning when she moaned. She'd had enough. "You were so good, sweetheart. Are you going to go against a direct order for your safety again?"

"God, I hope not."

He chuckled as he leaned down and kissed her hot globes. "Me too. I don't want to be here administering this type of spanking to your cute butt again. I much prefer this kind." He snaked his hand underneath her and rubbed her sopping wet pussy. "You are so damn wet, baby. I'm not sure I believe you've learned a lesson when you're this aroused. I can smell your perfume." He continued to massage, flicking her clit. She arched with the orgasm that slammed into her hard.

"Jac," she rasped after she'd crested the peak and had relaxed some. "I don't know if these feelings are love or simply lust but whatever it is, I'm so glad you feel it too."

"Charlotte, I love you. I don't just have some lustful feelings with nothing substantial to back them up. I. Love. You. I'll be right here while you work your own feelings out but never doubt mine for you."

He put his hands around her waist and helped her come up from her prone position. Her hot bottom was calling his name, and he intended on heeding the call.

"Go on upstairs, sweetheart. I'll close up and be right there, so get ready for me." She leaned over to turn off the lamp and got a slap for her trouble. A squeal accompanied her outraged expression.

"Do we need to repeat this little exercise in obedience? I said I'd do it."

"No need for a repeat, I was just helping."

"Thank you but you showing you understood my message by doing as I say is all I want right now."

"Whatever." He grabbed Charlotte by the waist, bent her slightly and landed four more substantial swats.

"Ow Jac, I promise I understand."

Jac shook his head and chuckled as she rushed up the stairs to the back of the house where the master suite was. He loved her snarky, sassy ways, but he intended she understood him in a way that meant something. She had to believe she needed to be more alert about her environment. He was afraid they weren't there yet. But they would get there. For now, he was going to get his girl's lips on his shaft.

SHARLEE RACED DOWN the hall and once inside the bedroom she headed straight for the bathroom. She was still achy for another orgasm and knew if she even tried, Jac wouldn't let her have one for days. She laughed at her thinking.

Honestly, she knew that if she really wanted to do it, she would, but she liked the boundaries. Sharlee craved his discipline because it meant someone, her lover, cared what happened to her. She didn't need some fancy degree to know she needed it—needed what only Jac could give her.

Sharlee had tried to analyze why she creamed when she thought of Jacquard Reynaud's deep voice, his stern looks, and his hard hand but she just knew he did it for her. She could tolerate Jac's irritation, dictatorial ways, bossy attitude, and rules but when he expressed disappointment in her, she almost died from sorrow. She craved his cuddles and his cock as well. This man just did it for her.

In the beginning, she'd tried to figure out why. She researched every site she could find, hacked into some major therapeutic clinics and a few universities, but while she found some reasons that a woman would look for a strong male partner, and why spanking held appeal and even where the thinking behind domestic discipline came from, she still came down to the same conclusion.

The whole package floated her boat, and that was okay.

After Jac was through with discipline, she knew the routine; bathroom, strip, wait. She'd read about the people who liked the higher protocol, but she didn't go in for all that. Luckily, Jac did, but on a lessor scale. He had learned quickly that while she would submit to his dominance and desires, she wouldn't be subjugated. She would not allow her spirit to be conquered. There was a big difference in her book and Jac understood that.

She heard his footfalls as he came closer to the bedroom. Sharlee sat on the edge of the bed, ready to do his bidding, not because he insisted, but because it pleased her to please him. She could still feel where his hand had firmly connected with her bottom. The bedspread was decorative but abrasive on her rear. She was determined to ignore the discomfort. She wiggled in anticipation.

Sharlee watched him stare at her from the doorway. He stripped slowly. She loved to undress him, but it seemed he either wasn't allowing her to as part of her punishment or he was too impatient to wait for her fumbling.

Jac strode into the room and when he was close enough, he held out his hand to her in invitation. Jac was all about permission and agreement. Even now, as he stood waiting for her move, she knew he would never force her. Her hand in his was permission. Even in discipline, he often asked for her concurrence. Sharlee placed her hand in his and he pulled her closer while he took his pleasure, placing light, insistent kisses on her proffered lips.

Sharlee shivered as he spoke against her ear in between kisses.

"I need your talented lips on my cock, sweetheart."

"Is that all I can touch?" She loved the game.

"Kiss down to him, then get out that pink tongue of yours to prep my cock before you take him inside your hot moist mouth. No hands. I want you to only use your mouth. I know you can do it. Show me you know how to follow orders."

"No hands?" the slap on her unsuspecting, still sore ass took her breath away. "I understand. No hands."

"Good girl." He patted her bottom and smiled when she hissed.

She was as much in fear of another swat as she was eager for the tingle his pat would bring. He was a tease in his own way, taunting her pleased him.

Following his instructions, Sharlee kissed and licked her way down his pecks, stopping to dance her tongue along his erect nipples before making a beeline for his belly button. She giggled against his naval as he flexed. Her tongue dipped inside and wiggled before continuing on.

She didn't realize he had swung down to catch her thigh until the swat landed. She answered it with a squeal and a rub.

"I'd remember that brats get punished, if I were you."

"That's mean. I'm trying to help you enjoy the journey."

Jac laughed. "Oh, I'll enjoy it no matter if I have to stop and paddle your ass again or if you simply follow my instructions like a good girl."

"Hmph. I guess I can just stick to the plan, but it won't be as fun."

"Oh, don't worry about that." He put his hand on the top of her head and directed her face towards his cock. "Open up."

She grinned. "Now the fun begins." He pushed his cock into her smiling mouth.

Sharlee twirled her tongue around his stalk and began the in and out motions mimicking what she hoped she would experience later that night. Jac knew she loved to lavish her attentions on his cock. The tingle of arousal was becoming more pronounced the longer she paid homage to the hardened, blood infused, purple flesh.

These days, she was easily excited. Simply knowing she was giving Jac pleasure was enough because she loved him. She could admit it to herself that no other man did the things to her psyche and her body that Jacquard Reynaud did. Her movements grew more intense to meet her body's needs and his. She tasted his precum and inhaled his scent. All thought was difficult as she concentrated on peaking and bringing him with her.

Suddenly, Sharlee was stopped by an insistent man as she deep throated him. She could not do it but as she drew back and buzzed his penis crown, carefully scraping her teeth along the length, his hand grabbed the sides of her head and stopped her.

She whimpered.

"Stop honey, I want to come deep inside you and if you keep working your magic for much longer, I won't be able to hold out."

Jac lifted Sharlee from her kneeling position on the floor where she'd finally landed, and kissed her lips as he placed her solidly on her feet. Sharlee looked bemused as she stood gaining her bearings. Jac was happy to help her get into position for him so he could light off the fireworks they both were so close to experiencing.

"Here sweetheart, get on your hands and knees."

Jac helped her into position. He reached down to find how close she was and found her drenched.

Sharlee moaned the wantonness his touch ignited.

He loved this woman. Jac loved bottom play of all kinds and he wondered if he could convince her of the adventures of butt plugs and more challenging backdoor play. He ran his finger through her wet center and spread some of her lubricating arousal to her bottom button. The scrunched brown opening retreated even tighter as his finger circled her crinkled skin.

"Have you had bottom play before, baby?" His finger continued to carry wetness from her center to her bottom.

"No and I'm not sure about it." Sharlee wiggled her rear to punctuate her statement.

"I can make it so good for you, you'll wonder why you ever waited so long. I'm glad you did. Wait, that is. I know it's selfish, but I love you will only experience that with me."

"But it will hurt and it's a little kinky."

Jac laughed at that as he pushed the tip of one finger inside her bottom with easy but continual pressure. "We are kinky, sweetheart."

"Huh. I don't feel kinky."

"You were getting yourself off while sucking my cock, you love spankings, and I'm about to show how you will love bottom play, so, yeah baby, you're kinky."

"Okay, I guess I'm kinky, but mmm, that feels good oddly. I feel kind of wiggly."

Jac swatted her bottom. "Yes, you are. Just know that we are going to start the exploration and it will get better than just my finger." Jac slid his digit out of her backside and teased her clit while he massaged his member. As Sharlee's arousal ramped up, her movements and cute little sounds of excitement grew more pronounced.

If he waited much longer his girl would fly before his cock could visit, so he removed his hand and slid home inside her hot, wet core. The little minx was precisely meeting his moves with some countermoves of her own. Spanking her made him happy, and she had suckled him so well he was relaxed and feeling generous. Since she was trying to take over the way they had sex tonight, he would allow her some freedom, but she would pay for the privilege with a reheating of her jiggling rear cheeks.

Each time Sharlee move her ass back to meet his forward motion, he would slap her bottom. After a few minutes of action, Sharlee stopped trying to control things, and he stopped reddening her bottom. Her cute sighs and achy moans were just what he needed to finish him off. Once he touched her bottom hole with his re-wetted finger Sharlee's orgasm slammed into her and his was only seconds behind. Yes, his girl would love some expanded bottom play and so would he.

Jac had been fortunate that Sharlee was on birth control, and he'd still hesitated to go bareback but Sharlee had shown him her last exam and with it was her birth control method. She should be good for another year according to her paperwork. She trusted him that he was clean, but he produced his checkup paperwork as well.

"Honey, not that I think you're not truthful nor do I think you believe that of me, but it takes the question away. I don't want to become a dad at this moment and I'm fairly sure you don't want to be a mom yet. And not to make you upset, but you tend to be a little haphazard in your personal affairs."

"Okay, so you're right there."

"All that being said, I had to prove I was clear after I had frequented certain establishments, so I have the document on hand. But I love that you trusted me."

That took care of that issue for ever, but something else was going on tonight. Sharlee was quiet. He pulled her into his arms and snuggled her close. "What are you thinking about?"

"I don't know. I guess I'm worried that this won't last."

"That what won't last, us?"

"Yeah, I mean, it's almost as though it is too good to be real. It's like we're burning so hot that we'll incinerate any day. I'm not sure I could recover from losing you."

"Oh, honey, we won't if both of us try to work extra hard to keep the lines of communication open."

"You mean not yell 'I quit' in the middle of a meeting and then storm out?"

"Good example. The whole room jumped down my throat. Evidently I was wrong." He smiled and Sharlee giggled. "But I don't explain myself often enough. I expect my orders to be carried out. I'm a military man and I run a shop with military guys in it. I promise to try not to order you about without an explanation if I can."

"And I promise to try not to take it personal if you can't."

He kissed her nose and then shimmied his way down to kiss her lips before continuing on to her neck, to her perky nipples, kissing each one before poising over the top of the right one. "See, we are already compromising and conversing. I'll communicate another way now."

His head lowered as his mouth strongly sucked on her breast. She arched into him and started her mews again. His cock nearly burst it had expanded so hard and fast. Time for round two.

God, he loved this woman.

Chapter 19

The weather had turned cold and rainy and instead of irritating them for a day or so, it had been nearly a week. Charlotte left the warmth of her bed early to work on another job, this one belonging to the teams. She loved her work, but it was so much easier when she worked from home and could take a nap during the day to make up for the loss of sleep the night before.

She loved being around Jac all day on most days but hated the time and schedule constraints working an outside job caused. She also hated it when Jac said enough, but she wasn't ready to stop. It was her work, and she should be able to choose her hours. He should understand the drive to finish the task well. And he did for himself and in theory for her too, but sometimes it just didn't translate well when he needed to give her the same consideration.

Sharlee asked about working at home a few times and Jac had tabled it citing the need to be able to access her immediately but now that he understood her work, she was going to push the point at the sitrep this morning. Jac had one every morning but sometimes only a couple reported, or everyone reported but had little to tell. Today was one of those quiet mornings. Sharlee opened the conversation.

"As you all know, this job that we do doesn't really have time constraints. I'm good with that, it's how I've worked for almost a decade now, but I need to be more flexible."

Monroe sat forward leaning his arms on the table. "How so?"

"Well, getting up and coming in at a certain time, going home at a certain time and trying to fit everything in what turns out to be a twelve-hour day, here. I feel like I'm on display." She indicated the fishbowl she worked in. It was like Jac's, with windows everywhere.

Garrett spoke. "You could go secure in the office. Turn on the smoke screen during the day."

"I guess. But getting up, dressed, and in the office to perform my job at a set hour every day is not how I've done it best. The time constraints cause another issue. When I've gone to bed at two a.m. then back here at eight can wear a person out fast. I can't do all the work here, well I could, but it would make for a number of long, sixteen-to-eighteen-hour days. Which I know you all object to unless you need something. I guess I want you to let me work from home more often—during the day. Not just at night."

Jac asked, "How often? Quantify it for me."

"Most of the time. Let me come in when you need me in the office, but I promise there is not one thing that I do here I can't do in China. Well, maybe not China with the unrest, but the point is I'm completely portable. Working all hours is killing me. I want to be productive here but sometimes the work isn't until the nine-a.m. crowd has gone to bed. Then I come in the next morning and just want a nap."

Carter clarified. "And you are more comfortable at home?"

"Yes, but not as in personal interactions. I'm good at home because I can stay in PJs if it's a long night and still work. If I'm tired and need a break, I can nap and then get up to check on my work. I can run to the store or even do a little stress relief in the gym if I need it."

Kaden asked. "Would you come in from time to time?"

"Absolutely. But on weeks like this, I could get so much more done, in a less stressful way, at home. And I would work less overall because I could adjust the schedule to only work when necessary. I can video conference you at any time."

Mark, who had remained silent as others chatted, spoke. "I think, since we all do things that help us work better, tighter, more efficiently, even taking part of the day off when we aren't needed, we have to understand what Sharlee is talking about. She's on all the time. Jac's on all the time. We have support staff for everything else. For me, Sharlee, if you want to work from home most of the time, I'm cool with it. Just expect us to drop in on you by computer or in person at any time." Jac grunted. "But there are obvious times we would call first," Mark amended with a grin.

"Yeah, I agree. We'll have to put up some cameras so that when Jac wasn't there, we could make sure you were safe," Garrett warned.

"Wait, like someone will just watch me work all day?"

"Don't even go there, Charlotte." Jac's voice held a warning.

Sharlee sat up straighter in her seat. "You know we have a cleaning lady. She could be a mole. We should do a deep background. Oh, right we already have someone monitoring the gates day and night, did we do a deep sweep on them or just the regular background. And your chef that is returning. You never know what he was doing in Florida with your parents."

"Keep it up, sweetheart. I'm going to love going home tonight." Jac's implication was clear.

Her sounds of disgust brought a few smiles that were quickly squelched.

"Jac, you have enough security?" Monroe asked.

Jac looked away from Charlotte. "Yep. And if we can beef things up equipment wise, like trick out the office, then I don't see any problem. I'm pretty much wired for sound everywhere else."

Kaden spoke. "Well, Sharlee, when we can get things in place and you are safe enough while working alone, I think we agree."

"Thanks guys. I know it'll be better this way. If not, I can rent a little apartment that I use on the heavy weeks."

"When hell freezes over, sweetheart and I wouldn't push it any further." Jac turned to encompass the room with a single glance. "We have some jobs to finish so let's get to it. Then we can concentrate on setting you up. Okay?"

"No problem."

It was the end of another week of late nights when things finally had the signs of settling down to a more naturally hectic pace. The guys were off to their weekend gigs or finishing their weekly gigs and Sharlee had just settled into her workspace to start what was supposed to be a short day of work when the fire alarm screamed.

After looking around to see if someone would say it was a false alarm with no positive result, she sighed and stood up. Becky was off today and Jac had gone out to a meeting. Mark was the floor monitor today. She grabbed her laptop and threw her purse strap over her head when Mark appeared at the door.

"Sharlee, move it. We'll lock the offices and gear remotely. This isn't a drill. There's smoke in the third-floor corridor. Let's hope the stairwell is clear enough for us to exit quickly."

"Where is everyone else?" she asked, as she allowed Mark to shuffle her into the stairwell.

"The staff followed the rules and left immediately. Everyone else is out of the office and I have all the spare keys so get going."

"Wait. My hand gun."

"Leave it. Hurry."

The fire engines arrived, the flame was stifled, and the building was cleared for reentry, except for the third floor. Sharlee continued back inside to resume working like the rest of the office building. She ran into Mark with a cut on his forehead and reached out to touch it.

"What happened to you?"

"Someone was going the wrong way to exit the building. We'll talk when we're in the office." Mark shuffled Sharlee in as he had shuffled her out, with purpose.

As Sharlee cleaned his cut Mark explained. "So I was going down the steps behind you when a man pushed his way through, heading up. I thought it was odd and followed him back to our floor and since, in a fire, our entry doors are unlocked to allow first responders in, he walked right in. I followed him, asked why he was there and got the coat tree tossed at me for my trouble." Mark indicated his head. "He took off right afterwards the way he had arrived and was lost in the crowd."

"Did you recognize him?"

"Nope."

"Think we have him on camera?"

"Hopefully, yes, he was in our waiting room when I reached him. He had a hoodie or something over his head though."

"You call Jac, and I'll take care of cueing the camera feed," said Sharlee. "Did everyone else get back in okay?"

"They did. Becky's two and Jessie and her bookkeeper. Four out, four returned."

Sharlee wondered, like Carter knowing about Becky's private life, how did Mark know Jessie's, but she couldn't stop to grill him today. She left Mark with two aspirins and went to her office. She unlocked the door, went straight to her desk, and started pulling up the video cams.

By the time people started returning to the office, she had isolated the whole incident. She did the best she could with side shot enhancements and sent the intruder's face through all the databases she had access to, waiting to see what would pop up. She knew it could take a while, and the guys weren't patient. After the sitrep and even though she said their intruder could have just been a common thief that figured he would try to snag something easy, they didn't believe it.

"Unfortunately, it appears deliberate. Otherwise, why even leave your own floor. That would be the easiest snatch and go," Kaden pointed out.

Garrett shook his head. "Only if he was the one responsible for clearing and securing the floor, otherwise he would have had to leave with the loot as others were leaving. Not conducive to good thievery."

"Sure," agreed Mark, "if he worked in the building. Something about him tells me he didn't. Look at how he was dressed, jeans and black tee. Not what the average person wears in this building."

Carter looked down at his clothes. "Well, all except the people on this floor I guess."

"Yes, well, that gets me back to the part about our accountant, Jessie, and Miss Charlotte."

All eyes focused on her but the only ones that bothered Sharlee were Jac's.

"Well, Jessie was sure she had circumvented me when I went through the first time. She was shutting things down, but since I now know her work saves in real time, I'm going to have a little talk with her about her choices. I might not give many orders around here," his eyebrows rose as he looked at Sharlee, "but when I say move, I expect to be obeyed immediately."

Time seemed to tick by slowly, but Sharlee jumped when Jac said, "Right, if you will handle Jessie, I'll handle Charlotte."

"Can I say something?" Sharlee's question was met with negative responses all around the table. "Fine but if I'm a full member of the team, why is it a big deal if I don't move when one of you snaps your fingers?"

Monroe stood as he spoke, "Sharlee, we've gone over this. We're protective of you. Yes, because you're a woman but also because you're our teammate. You have skills, but not the kind that can keep you safe if the real shit hits the fan. We don't let stupid things go by with anyone. You just get all of us instead of one or two at a time."

Kaden added, also standing, "You're also more sensitive to us jumping your a... butt."

"I have great personal defense skills and can shoot a bulls-eye almost every time. But you guys seem to forget that."

"We don't but if you come up against a guy with our skills, your personal defense won't be worth sh-poop," said Carter.

Sharlee stood, indignant and yet happy these guys cared enough about her to watch out for her. As she walked out the door Jac walked up behind her and spoke quietly.

"You know what to do when we get home."

"If I get there tonight, I'll think about it."

Jac chuckled, "Oh, you will because you aren't into public spankings. I don't mind them, and the guys are cool with them, so just let me know how you want to handle this." Sharlee left the conference room deciding she would go home, just not early.

Jac watched lustfully as his seductively dressed woman entered the room. They had been to this place a little more often lately. He loved her independence and her spirit, but her stubbornness would never end well. Here she stood, in her lace-covered, barely there panties and bra, and she was waiting for his punishment. He extended his hand. She took it. He pulled her onto his lap.

"Why are we here, sweetheart?"

"Because Mark tattled on me. But I really don't think I did anything wrong." Jac tried to hold back his grin. She was always spunky and sassy even when her butt was on the line.

"No, Mark would have had nothing to tattle on if you had left when you heard the alarm."

"Really, I was so deep into what I was doing I didn't even hear the alarm until just as Mark was coming in to drag me out."

"I see. Honey, that could be dangerous and with you wanting to work more often from home, it concerns me."

"I know I tune out the world, but I think that if there was a computer visual alarm, like a code only we know flashing on my screen, I'd immediately tune in."

"Can you set that up?"

"Sure, with Kaden's help to connect the two."

"Okay, then do it. Now, about today's incident—"

Her pout came out. "I don't think you should penalize me, Jac. As soon as Mark said something, I got up. I couldn't have done it any sooner."

Jac sat a moment before standing Sharlee back up. "Okay, so here's the deal. If you agree to the spanking, it won't be a punishment."

Sharlee's eyes sparkled, and her smile was full of lustful naughtiness. "Mmm, I could do that."

"Minx. I bet you can." He turned her around toward their bedroom, swatting her bottom solidly. He laughed at her squeal as she dodged the next swipe and raced for the bed.

Jac hoped he didn't make a mistake by giving her an out after he made a production of the spanking. This woman was going to be his forever if he had anything to do with it. He lay contentedly with her in bed, her soft breath tickling his chest hair and her sweet scent filling his nostrils, wishing he knew the answer to why she was targeted. He checked on the secondary safety plan.

He worried she was too vulnerable, too trusting of the goodness in life. Jac didn't want her to look for death around every corner, but he needed her to realize it could be around some corners and at least pay more attention. She was better, but was it enough? He kissed her soft, satiny hair and brought her in tighter. Sharlee whimpered and then snuggled in with a smile. Jac knew he would protect her with his life and so would his team. There was no better protection so why was he still worried? He always went with his gut, and it was still on alert.

Chapter 20

J ac spoke as he poured Sharlee's coffee into her travel mug. "I know that the pressure in the office is high this week but you're kind of testy this morning, sweetheart. Did you sleep well?"

"I'm doing the best I can, trying to keep up with everyone's demands, Jac. Some of the team's jobs are in their peak operative times right now. I'm allowed to be irritable trying to stay on top of the workload. And I'm still trying to locate the guy who broke into the shop."

"And how many outside jobs do you have, Sharlee?"

"A few, but I can handle them."

"How many?" His voice took her to her melting place, but this was her work, and she did it for herself as well as to maintain her connections, and keep her hand in the cyber pie. She lived for the thrill.

"Two. Just two because I turned down one I shouldn't have." Sharlee grabbed her computer bag and coffee. "We need to go."

Jac finished pouring coffee into his cup and grabbed his gear. Now that he had Sharlee with him at home, he did more of his PT there as well. He used the gym at work for stress relief. He had already grabbed clean training garb because he knew today was a gym day. Sharlee had been grumpy for several days and she was right, the heat was turned up. It would be helpful to stay focused if he hit the treadmill when he needed to clear his head.

He followed her out, set the alarm, and closed the door. At least her safety wasn't an issue any longer, and he slept better at night. Sharlee didn't go anywhere alone. Well, because of that and the sex they had often kept her close. His woman was eager to try new things and in the beginning it was all new, now she was asking for her favorites. He liked that. And he liked that one of those favorites was bottom play.

What he didn't like was the fact that she still took outside jobs. They had enough work to keep her busy and then some, but she continued to accept more work and then she found herself overtaxed which brought on her stress responses. All of which would earn her a hot seat if she wasn't careful. He had agreed she could continue partly because it was her choice really, and partly to save the relationship but sometimes he wondered if he had backed down on the wrong issue.

She refused to believe that if she let go of the other contracts that she'd have enough work. That's what she said but Jacquard knew the real reason. She wanted backup in case things didn't work out at the company, with him. Her faith in them wasn't strong enough yet. But he had to try to lessen her load. She was submissive in the bedroom so maybe if he pushed, she'd submit to him on this. They had agreed on exercising the compromise and communication muscle. It was time to put it into action.

He climbed into the driver's seat and leaned over to buckle Sharlee in.

"I can do it, Jac."

"I know. I just like to do it."

"Thanks."

"I hate to see you so stressed. Is there anything I can do to help?"

"I appreciate it, really, I know I'm much more irritable when I'm in the high-pressure zone, but you can't help more than you have. I just need to work on things and let the guys finish the task."

"The extra jobs—"

"Jac, please don't harp on those again. I listened to you and turned down a contract. I wish I hadn't but there it is. Please don't ask more of me."

Jac nodded. "Okay, but if things get out of hand—"

"You'll bring yours into play, I know."

"So long as we're clear."

"We are."

Jac patted her leg but knew something else was going on. He simply couldn't figure out what. Silence reigned for the rest of the trip.

By the time they arrived through some tougher than normal morning commute traffic, Sharlee was antsy again. She allowed him to open her door, but she huffed at the inconvenience. His baby was going to find him more responsive than she expected soon if she didn't shut down the attitude. They entered the elevator, and he hit the stop button in between the floors, walking her into the corner of the car.

"If you need a spanking to calm things down, I'm willing to do that right now so the rest of your day is smooth."

"No. I'm sorry I'm moodier, but I can handle this. It will get better when we shift me and my office home."

He loved when she called the house they lived in home. "You need to remember that if I see you're having difficulty, I'll take over."

"I'll be fine. I promise and thank you for taking care of me, and I don't mean in that way. I think we should go up now. We are awfully busy."

His kiss began light and gentle, encouraging her response. By the time he had lifted his head, he knew he'd be working with a hard on and his lady would be slick with arousal. Her enlarged pupils and shallow breathing assured him she was just as affected as he was. Whether they'd make it to the end of the day before combusting was yet to be seen. While she wasn't the most submissive woman he had ever been with, Sharlee was the most enticing one.

He'd been with his share of women, but none that excited him or got under his skin in the same way as this one did. At times, he wanted inside her more than he wanted his next breath. Charlotte Hope Armstrong was a brat. He loved her independence, but it got her into trouble sometimes. Now with their change in relationship status, he could address it like he had wanted to from the first time she had gotten flat tires off the main road when disregarding the rules. He'd introduced her to his discipline then. She craved it now. She was a gem, and he planned to go slow and careful to make sure that she was ready to progress to the next step of their journey, whatever that was.

The home office was almost set up, and the security was in place, but they were waiting on a few last pieces to call it official. Sharlee was in the shop at the start of the second hard week in a row. Her assistance on deep web diving for information included hooking up with some of her contacts. It was frustrating because Jac said it wasn't safe. Safe or not, she'd done it and got what she needed for the team.

That was her job, and she was good at it. The rest of the team did their things that were not always considered safe, far from it. But she used discretion and had been extremely careful so far. Sharlee could find the needle in a haystack, thread it, and sew the access closed before anyone knew the hole existed.

Just this morning, as a start, she closed all bank transfers involving an international drug dealer after she had disbursed all the funds to benevolent societies as an anonymous donation and she'd only had one cup of coffee. She was amazing.

One of her outside jobs, however, was a different story. She'd worked on opening access and securing the multiple participants cyber links for video connections to the conference. That had been last week. The job had been easy. Connect these entities for video chat, stay on while they did their talk, close the secure access and sever ties and trails that linked them.

But it didn't work like that.

Sharlee had accepted the job from a senator the team had assisted earlier in the year. She'd gotten them through the talks but when she tried to sever the links, one particular link wouldn't disengage. She could disconnect her link, but she could not do the same for the two parties, the party from Africa and the party from the Middle East. This was the second time she had experienced trouble with this senator and one of his conferences.

The first incident involved a munching Trojan virus launched by one of the parties left on at the end. The virus had been launched, and both parties disconnected immediately. She could take care of it, but she was surprised. Like last time, she explained the situation to her contact, and he was furious with her, stating she had falsely advertised her expertise.

That made her angry and by the time she was done, she had disconnected them, placed both participants on some high-profile watch lists, had sicced the tax people on the contact and sent her bill to the conference organizers with a hefty irritation fee.

After lunch that same afternoon, Sharlee was uncovering some major players for Carter and Mark. Kaden was her side-kick when it fit into their schedules for hardware set up. He didn't love the programing and security deep diving like she did, but he was interested enough to gather some information and he was a wiz on the hardware side.

Later that night, Carter tried to go to the site he watched her access earlier, just to see if he could do it. Immediately a virus was released on his home computer which was unprotected by Sharlee's firewalls and barriers. She laughed when he called her at home. She was just reading another advertisement on how to avoid ever getting a virus again. Carter needed to read more and access less.

She laughed again the next morning. "And the take home message here is, never go deep and never access sensitive documents outside your protective bubble. Now go away while I scrub your machine."

It had taken all morning to eradicate the intruding programs, a morning that was already full. Carter apologized with coffee and donuts. Now, it was lunch and this time she noticed before it was midafternoon. She had finally slipped out to the cafeteria to grab a bite to eat, something she knew would make her bossy boyfriend happy, but some moron was shadowing her every move. Or at least she thought so. She looked around multiple times but found no one.

It was probably nothing but combined with the realization that the virus that had invaded and implanted some odd data on Carter's machine was in a Trojan, it was concerning. The virus was like the one sent to her at the senator's conference the first time and Carter had gone onto that same international site.

It was probably nothing, she told herself again, but she learned to listen to her instincts as the guys had taught her and her gut said something was not right. She took one last look on her way back but saw no one. She shrugged and climbed the stairs to the office. That should count as exercise today, she thought, as she shook off the odd feeling. It was gone now. She was sure it was overwork that made her jittery.

She hadn't left the building because she promised she wouldn't without escort. The whole office was out more often than they were in these days, save the support staff, and her. She was both support and a team member. But she wanted to be home working in her bare feet.

She smiled when she thought of Jessie, the accountant. She wanted to ask her how Mark handled her naughtiness, but figured Jessie and Mark might not appreciate it. Nonetheless, she saw Mark make more trips to check on things in the other office and she was pretty sure Jessie had taken to using hers and Rebecca's bathroom instead of the one closer to her office because she wanted to get a glimpse of him. Yep, when things calmed down, she would get to know Jessie better.

"Well, if I have to be here until they set things up, then I'm doing it my way," she murmured to an empty office.

Sharlee kicked off her shoes and turned on her music. She smoked the windows, took off her jacket, turned up the heat in the room and got cozy on her sofa. She was finally making some real progress when Rebecca spoke through the intercom. That woman had suddenly decided she wanted to be called Becky by everyone, not just girlfriends. Charlotte wondered if the guys had finally gotten to her.

"Yes, Becky?" She had tried not to sound as irritated as she was but knew she had only been minimally successful.

"Sorry, Char, um, Miss Armstrong, I know you're busy but no one else is here, and the visitor refuses to leave until he speaks to someone."

Sharlee looked at the camera feed and thought there was something familiar about the man, but she couldn't put her finger on exactly what it was. "Can you take his name, number and find out what he wants?"

"I asked, but he didn't want to give any of it."

"Well, then he doesn't want to speak to anyone bad enough. Tell him I am unavailable. He can sit until a partner comes back if he likes. That's fine with me."

Before she knew it and before she got off the phone with Becky, he had pushed his way through the outer office door, into the entry hall and Becky had hit the alarm. The camera in the office showed Sharlee as he tried the office door, but it automatically locked when Becky hit the panic button, trapping him in between the inner and outer office in the small reception walkway. It left Becky in her outer office and Sharlee in the inner one with both doors and the entrance doors locked. God, she loved working for a security firm. She knew Becky's desk would move and reception's as well after this.

The police showed up, at the same time her phone rang. Jac. Once the intruder was cuffed, Becky explained what happened to the officer. Sharlee verified the story and copied the tape for them. Still no name by the time the cops took him away. After getting off the phone with Jac, she closed up the office sending everyone home after the police had gone.

Sharlee hadn't brought her car, so she took a cab back to her comfy clothes and wine. Jac might be upset, but she was done for the day, and she knew poor Becky was, too. And Sharlee couldn't get rid of the feeling she recognized the man from somewhere.

Charlotte was getting a little worried when the camera kicked on and she watched Jac enter the property.

"Hi baby, sorry you had to come home alone. I never meant that to happen but with the security detail we were running and the early closing of the office, which was a good call, I couldn't get to you at the right time."

"I know. I understand, but poor Becky probably shouldn't be alone."

"Carter offered to make sure she was doing okay." Jac said, and then kissed her.

"Mark should check on Jessie."

"Shit, Charlotte, who else should we check on?"

"No one. Everyone else has someone to look in on them."

Jac leaned down and cupped the back of Sharlee's head, slipping his fingers behind her neck and threading them upwards, anchoring them in her hair.

"You're amazing, do you know that?"

He held her tight, drawing her in closer as he deepened the kiss. Sharlee needed the stress relief.

"Jac, make love to me."

That was all the opening he needed. "Take your clothes off."

She hesitated for too long and the sting on her thigh told her he was not repeating himself. She shook her head. "I need you to do it."

Something in her eyes must have told Jac he needed to take care of his girl. Coddle and comfort her like she rarely asked for but when she needed it, she really needed it. He slowly and gently took her restrictive clothing off. She'd kicked off her heels when she walked in but the rest waited for his fingers to release her from them.

Loving the feel of his hot body on hers, Sharlee gave as good as she got, taking the initiative to run her hands over his butt and squeeze. Immediately there was the familiar sound of slapping and a sting on her flank, below her left hip.

"Ow, Jac." She whimpered.

"I'm in charge here. Or did you forget?"

"I sort of did. Can't I at least use my tongue?"

Jac took her lips hostage invading her mouth with his tongue, enticing the dual and satisfaction of the battle. He nibbled her skin before swinging her up in his arms to take her to the bedroom.

"Let's go use your tongue."

Sometime later, hot, sweaty, and sated, they lay in each other's arms. After a short nap, Jac asked about what happened that afternoon. As she was explaining and remembering that strange thought she had about knowing the intruder, she recalled the feeling that someone was following her. She jerked up in the bed, almost bouncing on her knees.

"That's it! He was the man from the apartment. I wonder if he was the one following me today. I bet, if Mark looks, he'll find he was the man from the fire alarm day, too."

Jac sat up quickly next to her reaching for her arm. "What man? Who the hell was following you and why am I just hearing about it?"

"Well, I'm not sure who he was but..."

When the story had been told, Jac was on the phone calling Garrett and having Sharlee pull surveillance tapes. Sharlee sighed. *At least I got my orgasms first.*

Chapter 21

Several long hours later, Sharlee had fallen asleep in Jac's lap refusing to go to bed without him. The guys had headed home. They would look into things while Sharlee did her further research and digging, but Jac knew she had to agree to tighter controls. His girl would fight but he would counterattack. He loved her more than he ever thought possible and that meant there was nothing too intensive to keep her safe.

Jac was still shocked at the strength of emotion he had for this mouthy girl with strawberry blonde locks and green eyes. He would die to protect her and even though she didn't want to admit it yet, he knew she felt the same. She said love but not in the way she would soon. His girl was ferocious when she saw injustice, or she needed to protect someone but didn't turn that focus inward when it was her who needed protecting.

She had done her own version of an Alpha Charlie when she found out that Mark was not easy on Jessie. Mark didn't disclose what he'd done but had told Sharlee in no uncertain terms that it was his business, and she had no part of it. Sharlee would find out soon, he was sure. Jac chuckled remembering the stand-off. If it had been most women being that familiar with him, Mark would have laid into her ass, but Sharlee was off limits now that she was with Jac. And they both knew it.

He whispered as he took her to bed, "Okay baby badger, time to go to bed."

The next morning, when Charlotte saw some of the team she asked those assembled, "When do I get my office at home? Aren't you guys done yet?"

Monroe said it first. "I don't think it's safe for you to be on your own right now, especially after yesterday."

"What? No, I'm done with that crap. You all promised." She looked at Jac and Garrett.

"Yes, we did, but that was before someone tried to get to you at lunch and then in the office yesterday," Garrett responded standing to get more coffee.

"I'll have feeds, phones, locks, and all sorts of bells and whistles. You even have a freaking front gate guard. You need to let me go or I'll go before you're ready."

"Fine," growled Jac, "but you wait until Friday. The guys will have everything installed and tested by Friday.

"Fine." But she wasn't fine.

The group disbursed, but when Sharlee tried one of her databases from other channels, they denied access. She found a backdoor, but that had never happened before and when she called to find out why, they refused her call. She'd hit a brick wall, pounded it really, s. Someone was trying hard to cause her to lose her contracts. Or worse, to discredit her.

Whichever it was, she needed to bury herself and bring in the hole after her so as to leave no trace. She wondered if the cartoon bunny that did that cute scene of folding up his hole and pulling it inside its invisible pocket knew about the world of cyberspace before it even existed.

When Charlotte was hidden, the Vaper went in. She was determined to find out who did what to cause this trouble. She worked furiously, opening pathways and then removing any trace of her trail. Sharlee had gotten lax, and people got dead that way. She would not make that mistake again.

She was still erasing her trail as far back as she could go and furiously chatting with some off-the-grid contacts to help her find the source when Jac walked in.

"I need the situation reports when you have them for yesterday. And I think you have a few more the guys left with you. I'm on my way to a meeting. I'll bring back lunch."

He leaned down to kiss her, but Sharlee wasn't having anything to do with that. She divided her attention further to finish the reports. The fact that she had to devote some time to another task made her angrier than earlier in the day if that was at all possible.

She had nowhere to put the feelings.

Grabbing the guys' paperwork off the shelf and hers off her desk she stomped into her lover's office. Instead of placing them on Jac's desk neatly, she tossed them in the direction of his desk not caring when they fell to the floor around his chair. She needed something only Jac could give her, and he wasn't even there to take care of her. She tipped his desk chair over before storming to the bathroom.

When she walked out of the restroom, she heard him call out from his office. "Damn, sweetheart, now?"

Suddenly she didn't want to push him and the relief she had desired just moments ago was no longer something she wanted. She ignored him and began banging on her keyboard. A beefy male held his hand in front of the screen, Jac's hand.

Palm up. She tried to look around it, tried to move it out of the way but it was immoveable.

Her tummy jumped and flipped. She salivated. She swallowed. Even her heart sped up noticeably. Finally she sighed, looked up and to her left. She saw his face, steady and kind. She had asked for his help, and he was giving it.

"I'm fine, Jac. Things have just been a little tough these last few weeks and I want my home office." His hand remained steady, waiting for hers. It made her chest ache.

"Really, it's good. Sorry I threw those reports on your desk. I'll clean them up. And pick up the chair."

His hand was still there. She looked up at him again and he dipped his head in a half nod indicating his hand.

She really wanted to, needed to, but...

"Do it, sweetheart. Put your hand in mine and I'll take care of the rest. Let me help you feel better."

That was all it took. She sniffled. Her tears silently flowed. She placed her hand in his and the decision was made.

JAC LED HER INTO THE office, hit the darkening button, shut and locked the door. She wore a cute skirt with flounces that day, no pencil skirts for his girl. Pulling the leather quirt out of his side drawer, he looked into Sharlee's eyes when he heard her sharp intake of breath. She recognized it from one of Jac's earlier introduction sessions only she had been standing and leaning over the side of the sofa.

"You need this baby. You've been worried, scared, angry, tired, frustrated, and about half a dozen other things these last weeks. It's made you sullen, grumpy, and downright hard to live with. You need me to fix things. Lean over, honey. You'll feel better."

Tears that were already making their way down her cheeks fell faster. "But that leather thing will hurt."

"Quirt, it's called a quirt, and I promise not to use it more than I need to. More than you need me to. Just enough to relieve you. It's stingy but I've had it modified for over the lap use. Now crawl over and get into position. I'll warm you up first."

"Can't I just have a regular spanking?"

"Charlotte Hope, who is it that determines the particulars of your spankings?"

"You, but I asked for this one."

"And if you don't want a punishment spanking, and trust me you are close, you will do as I say and quit stalling."

She hesitated.

"Baby, I'm trying to help." Jac's voice held an almost pleading quality.

She went over his knee. He flipped her skirt and lit her southern cheeks on fire quick as lightning. She cried at the sudden onslaught. He slapped her bottom with his hand repeatedly, so fast she couldn't count the smacks if she wanted to. She was nearly choking in the flood of tears.

Jac changed positions to give him more space. The double leather tongues made contact with her already sizzling backside. She squealed. Her tears fell as fast and furious as the spanking, but when he was done and her tears had subsided, sitting in his lap filled her up with contentment and security.

He'd fixed it as he promised. It was that simple. No matter how mad or frustrated she got, Sharlee knew Jac was it for her. He didn't have to convince her any longer, she was a convert.

JAC DIDN'T KNOW WHAT to think. He'd just sent three guys and the building security to disengage the alarms. Did they trigger all the alarms on their cars coincidentally at the same time this morning? And was it a fluke that someone tried to break into the offices not once but twice? And how about following Sharlee and ransacking her apartment? And what about that sorry excuse of a man, Kyle?

They arrested the man and charged him with criminal trespassing before releasing him. His name didn't ring any bells with anyone, and all Sharlee had under that name was what they all could easily get. Was he the man responsible for all the incidents? She was adamant there was more. Jac had just given her permission to dig further even though he didn't think she had waited for his okay.

But she pretended well.

"That isn't his real name, obviously, but finding it will not be easy. I'm working on it," she said from her home office that Jac was now becoming worried about. He thought he should work from home more often these days till they figured things out.

Sharlee expressed her frustration that he had not been arrested before. "I need to get his fingerprints."

"No, you aren't hacking the cops, young lady, and I say we should look at some of our other issues to see if they are connected."

"Jac, you're no fun. Okay, look, I didn't tell you something that I probably should have."

"Charlotte Hope, I think you should first go get the implement of your choice for the after party."

Sharlee rolled her eyes. "No, really, it's about the last outside contract I finished. I tried to use the database, and it denied me entrance."

"That makes sense, hon, you'd finished the job."

"I keep access between jobs because they don't want to wait while the paperwork processes each time. I can get in and out and finish several contracts in the time it takes the paper to emerge on the other side. And that's if I make it work with a little cyber help." She wiggled her fingers and her eyebrows.

Jac shook his head. "So what you're telling me is that they took away your access."

"Right and they refused my calls. That's never happened."

"Well, guess you don't take any more contracts from them. It doesn't hurt my feelings."

"Well it should. So, I backtracked the email system and found a few things out."

"I thought you couldn't get in."

"I said they denied me access, not that I couldn't get in. I just never had to use the rear entrance."

"Well, you like backdoor play." It was Jac's turn to wiggle his eyebrows.

"Shut it and be serious. It took a few days, but I found out what happened. The middle man between me and the department I deal with had sent emails that indicated I was releasing top secret information. He states it is to a Middle Eastern contact and an African contact that do not agree with the U.S. policies towards them."

"Gotcha. So now what?" asked Jac as he leaned back in his seat.

"He told them in an email that he had proof, but I don't see that he has produced it so I could help him produce nothing," said Sharlee with a smile.

"Okay because there isn't any how are you going to change that outcome? And do you plan to respond legally? And what would be this guy's motive? And who is this middleman?"

"My job is on the line and most likely the motive. See, I negotiate my own contracts, and most don't. The middleman gets a cut of the money and it's nothing to sneeze at. But that's not all. I think there's information on the loose, but it isn't being leaked by me. I just need to find out what it is and who leaked it. Then I share that info."

"So just tell the contractor."

"Jac, aren't you listening? I can't. He won't take my calls."

"What're you going to do about it? If he won't take your calls then..."

"Find the SOB and fix his wagon, of course."

"No, Charlotte. It's too dangerous."

"No, it's more dangerous if I don't because I'll be disposable. And it will also compromise your business with any government entity."

"Shit. I told you to get rid of the contracts. You're going under until this threat has passed."

"Jac, I know how to go deep. I didn't give them any addresses ever."

"Yeah, then how did he know where your apartment was?" Jac was so agitated he was walking his home office parameter.

She shook her head slowly. "I can't answer that. We need to set this up right. Call the guys."

Jac never disclosed what he and Garrett had done prior to opening this business, and he hadn't intended to let it out. But if Charlotte were in trouble, then he would pull out every damn contact they all had to keep her safe.

Jac didn't call the guys to come to his house. He sent them to Monroe's. Since Garrett's girlfriend had moved out, Jac had first thought to go there, but Garrett didn't answer until later. Monroe said there was no reason to put his house on the map in case Callie came back and they needed to keep her out of any fray. Jac agreed. Garrett was half a man without her, so if she came back, they promised amongst themselves to help him keep her.

"And this time, that man better tie her to his bed and put a ring on her finger," said Mark.

Carter nodded. "Agreed. When we're done with this, maybe we could toss a wide net and see if we can bring her in."

Monroe grunted. "Sounds good. See you in a few."

Jac wanted to leave Sharlee at home, but he didn't dare, and he couldn't bring the guys to her because he was going to tighten the security even further and leave a man with her at all times. She was going to hate that. He didn't care. Jac made the call.

He set Sharlee up in the corner of the room, digging for things they needed as they discussed strategy. Whenever she found a name or contact they were searching for, she added it to her document and by the time she had finished, some very high-ranking people were on that list.

"Now, we need a schedule for watching over Sharlee," directed Monroe and Carter held up his paper, mapping out the times they would need to cover.

"No way." Sharlee stood as she spoke. "I'm not a child to be babysat."

"No, you are a team member and my woman, so you will sit down, in my lap if you like, and either contribute intelligently or stay quiet and let us do it, but it is going to happen."

Jac was not a man to be argued with or cajoled when he was in this type of mood. She crawled into his lap and fell silent while they worked on the schedule. He rapped her up in his arms and leaned back while listening and giving his input.

"I have pulled from another team who is on standby. He is recovering from bruised ribs but is fine to hang out if we need him to."

Sharlee sat up and Jac cringed as he quickly resettled her in a different spot of his lap. Sharlee grinned.

"I don't like it, but I'll agree to it. But the minute I fix this, the watchdog duty is done, right?"

"The minute we can call you safe, then your security detail will be over. And the rest of the team will determine if you're safe, not you. Now, let's go home, baby."

The security upgrade was going into play. And Jac determined he was going to look into a new building that he could better secure as soon as this threat was over. He wasn't ever going to compromise on the safety of his people because he was in a shared business space again.

Chapter 22

Taking a leaf from Jac's book, Sharlee assembled all of her information on a wall in the home office. Jac used a whiteboard and erased it daily. He said it was safer to take a picture and review it later. He hated to worry about anyone in his office, even support staff, getting the wrong information without providing it for them. She didn't have that concern in their home office.

Standing back to get a general overview after she placed everything, she felt something niggling in the back of her mind but like the word you couldn't quite conjure up from the edges of your mind, the thought was elusive. She went to get coffee.

Jac walked into the office drying his hair and perused the wall of controversy, her situation board. Sharlee came in behind him, sipping from her cup.

Sharlee made a concerned noise behind him. "It looks nice, but I can't figure out what I'm missing. It's right there on the edge of my mind but it refuses to step all the way in."

"Okay, let's talk it through." Jac lifted his finger and walked it through the air as he touched off the connections. "Okay let's figure out what we know by working backwards through the incidents."

"I have done that, but maybe you saying it out loud will trigger that thought I can't quite get to." Together they traced each incident and each job to their common denominators.

"Okay, so the only job you did that involved the Middle East or Africa at all, was that conference for the senator."

"Yeah and I had trouble only at the end. I mean, I did have a conference with all the same players before but there weren't any problems."

"Okay, and your clients or contractors don't talk to you directly?"

"You know, it's like here. I'm just a part of the puzzle and things go through their personal assistants or seconds. I speak to the one who pays the bill only twice, when they open and then close the contract. I ask all the questions in the opening and the client asks all the questions at the end."

"So, he didn't have any questions on this job?"

"No, well, if he did, I didn't know about them because this one was odd. I only dealt with the aide. I mean I'd done so many contracts for this department and I've had several with this specific entity, I just took on the job. It was one I'd done many times before. Routine. So I never spoke to him."

"Then who set up the contract?"

"His aide. And the aide closed it too because I couldn't get the, um, contractor on the phone."

"So, for all intents and purposes, anyone could have been doing this conference outside of the normal source. It didn't even have to be a contract from the Senator. You don't know because you didn't connect with him this time."

"Well, sure, I guess."

"Was this usual?"

"Never, but I needed to do a more thorough report because I couldn't talk to the contractor." Sharlee stood concentrating intently at the board. "Jac, I'm so stupid. The Middle Eastern connection and the African connection, I get it now. The conference I monitored and hooked up had them in it. Not odd but they were the two that didn't disengage when everyone else did."

"Did you let the organizer know?"

"I complained about them to the contract person but actually, I had to leave the information with his aide, er, personal assistant. I never spoke to the sen—gentleman. His assistant asked for more information, so I put it all in the report and emailed everything to both the aide and the contractor. Wait. It was the aide. He set everything up for the conference and set me up. The senator never knew about it, did he?"

"Probably not. And the only recent job we did with those nationalities was Nnamani and that was supposedly for the senator, but he only signed our paperwork. I guess I never noticed because Nnamani and a different official signed. That is a connection. I spoke to a personal assistant as well."

"Like my contract," said Sharlee.

"The only job we did for the senator that the senator was personally involved in was the security detail for him and his family for a week. And other than that minor blip you had a question on once, which turned out to be nothing, there was no problem."

"Hot damn, now I know where to look." Sharlee sat at her computer monitors.

"Have you ever seen this aide before?" asked Jac.

She shook her head. "Nope, and I googled him but nothing much came up, no pictures. Now I can finish this. I'll find his picture, just give me a few."

"Charlotte, do not leave the house."

"But Jac, I like to get some fresh air and if I find out what I need, I'm hacking in and contacting the right people. It might mean I have to make a personal appearance."

"If you want fresh air, I'll be home to take you later. Do. Not. Leave. There is not one good enough reason for you to disregard my words. Personal contact is not happening."

"Whatever. You don't get it."

"Charlotte!"

"Got it, got it, I won't leave. But I have to work now. I have a man to find."

"Not personally. You never connect personally, and you aren't starting now. Locate but do not pursue. Leave that to me."

"You know that is the same thing in my line of work," asked Charlotte. Her snarky attitude was pushing it and she knew it.

"You do know that if you leave this house unprotected and without authorization, there won't be anything to save your ass from becoming the new version of red light therapy."

There was nothing yielding in her man's face or demeanor, and she understood. He was frightened she wouldn't be safe enough, and she'd get into a mess he couldn't get her out of fast enough.

"Yes sir, I promise." She reached up and kissed him. "Besides, he wouldn't be the one that did anything like break into my apartment. That's chump work next to what he does. He couldn't afford to jeopardize his job. It's his only access to the other corruption. But you'd be surprised what a girl with my skill set could do to a man in his position."

"These guys are playing hardball, honey, the kind of game where the loser dies."

"You have my word I won't put myself in danger. When I have something, I'll let you know."

He stared at her for a moment before nodding. "Carter is here this morning."

"Oh, but Monroe was on the schedule."

"He had something to do. Carter was working on his reports, so he'll do them here."

"Glad we bought food."

Jac kissed her again and left to get ready to go to the office.

THE DAY WAS QUIET AS Sharlee worked on gathering intel. Now that she knew what she was looking for, her searches were more fruitful. Her paths were more directed, so she could connect them. Finally, she matched the aide Craig Headley, and the two participants from Africa and the Middle East that she had worked with earlier.

Lo-and-behold, she found connections to the job Jac had undertaken with her senator. She had known at the time that it was the same senator, but she couldn't share the information. He was asking for a deep protective sweep because he thought someone on his long list of enemies was after him. They vetted as much as they could. Now Sharlee knew it was the senator's own aide that was the rat fink.

So now she wondered who had suggested Jac be the one to do the job with Nnamani but was pretty sure she had already identified who it was. They needed to get to her computer and download or upload things and possibly leave behind evidence that would say she was a link they had to sever, permanently. As she compiled her information to show Jac, Carter walked in just as a picture flashed on the monitor.

Carter pointed to the screen. "He was sitting in a car outside the office when I left today."

"Call Jac and tell him to lock it down. We have to get to the office."

She had a way to protect her information and used it daily. Today was no different. Sharlee locked it all up in two clouds, sent it to Jac's office, remotely blocked her office computer and put her laptop in the walk-in safe, adding Jac's to the stack of things he kept inside.

She had pulled the hard drive from her new CPU and since she hadn't had time to set it up fully, there wasn't anything on there to worry about. Sharlee pulled it and put it in the safe, too. She unlocked the gun safe and pulled out her own weapon. She threw it in her bag along with a laptop that she used in public.

"Let's go." Carter pulled his gun and led the way to the garage.

After locking things up and setting the alarm, Sharlee went to the passenger front seat.

"No, lie in the backseat and stay down."

"But why?"

"Think about it. We can't have you seen leaving in case someone is watching for you."

She hesitated and then agreed, sliding into the large SUV and onto her belly on the seat. She knew the dark windows would probably be enough, but she promised to do what she could to stay safe.

"Hey, this isn't the way to the office."

"No, not directly, but I am taking a short tour. Jac has gotten some information as well. He's handling the office, but we have to be positive you aren't being followed. Everyone is called in and the security is going to be high. I'm giving them time to make it happen."

"Smart." Soon they pulled into what sounded like a garage.

"Don't get out or lift up until I get you. I have to make sure they're ready for us."

She heard a door open and almost sat up but tried to do as she was told to stay safe. The door opened and Carter's huge body shielded hers as he pulled her out and walked them forward. Soon she was inside, and Carter released her. The environment disoriented her as she looked around in enough time to see Carter shut the door.

"Carter! Wait, what's going on?" Racing toward the door, its loud clang spoke of the thickness. Carter's voice came through a wall com.

"Sorry, Sharlee but you'll be okay. I promise you won't have to stay here long. You'll be safe until I get back. There's food, drink, and a bathroom. Actually, you could live in there, but I promise you won't have to."

Then he was gone. *What the hell had just happened? Why did Carter leave me here? Please don't let Carter be one of the bad guys.*

Charlotte you trust him.

Jac trusted him, everyone liked him. No, something else had to have happened. Sharlee tried her cell phone, but it didn't work inside this rich man's tomb.

Okay, Charlotte Hope Armstrong lets figure this thing out.

Taking slow careful stock of things, Sharlee knew that someone wouldn't have something so advanced and not outfit it with the latest technology. She touched every panel and opening, every door, no matter how small. Finally, in a little cubby, she tapped around until the spring-loaded latch popped open revealing a control panel. She systematically touched every switch and watched what it did. The fourth button triggered a wall panel. The wall covering pocketed away into the ceiling and another control panel rolled out.

"Just like the movies," she observed to an empty room. "Cool. I need Jac to get me one of these."

The thought sobered Sharlee. She had no idea what was happening outside of her solitary confinement, and she needed to find out. Sitting in the seat that was attached to the compact control panel, her fingers clicked away hoping she would get the expected result. If anything in her present world could be counted on it would be her knowledge of technology. She didn't have time to deal with much of a learning curve. After a few false starts, she could finally use the system to find the override logistics. This was an incredible system. If only she had time to appreciate it to its fullest potential. But she didn't. She opened another screen and followed the senator's aide as he continued on his reign of invasion.

Using a second screen, Charlotte tried to tap into the office cam.

The office came up quickly because she had the information to access it. Strange, no one was around. Something must have happened. She checked the support offices. No one. No, wait. Was that Jessie under her desk? Is that where everyone was—hiding? She panned the camera. No, it looked like only Jessie. Holy... Someone was trying to commandeer her cameras.

Sharlee quickly changed the access codes and regained control but whoever did that was in her realm of skill. She locked the access points on the cameras and made every false attempt at another source to create a release of little viruses. That should keep him or her busy for a while. She changed avenues because she couldn't afford for her access to be compromised by tracing back to the source. She re-routed the trail disbursing the signals then shut it down at the source and created an alternative path.

Something must have kept Jessie under the desk. Sharlee scanned the entry and found two people locked in the inner entry, like the man who had tried to get inside when she'd been in the office alone. Someone was walking into her office. She was glad she had shut her system down and locked it remotely. Now she sent a self-destruct command on it. If anyone happened to access her system, it would do an immediate crash and burn killing any further ability to touch her information.

The other window had stopped processing. There he was, in the cyber flesh, Craig Headley. This was her chance to dump what she knew before people way above her pay grade gagged it. She sent a flood of all her gathered information to the press agencies, the senate house, the other aides, the representatives, the White House and then she broadcast it to every computer in the office. The picture showed him, and the word WANTED emblazoned across the front. Then to the entire office building she sent a flash that said he was in the building. *Please exit with extreme caution.*

That was when the cameras in the office went down. His computer guy must have decided that to shut down any camera access was better than figuring how to control them. Smart move. Unfortunately now, Sharlee still didn't know where anyone was except Jessie.

"Don't move Jessie. Mark will find you," she said to the still empty room.

Stopping to think what she could do about getting out of this steel trap, she put Headley on the watch list of every organization she could access quickly. She sent his location to the local police and a few other places. She listed his known associates and let the system do the rest. Now she'd access the room exit sequence and get the hell out of dodge.

Chapter 23

The new air, stale as it was in this small underground garage compared to the high-tech room with its premium air exchange system, spoke of freedom. Hailing a cab was out of the question in this residential neighborhood. She couldn't identify whose house this was, but she was pretty sure it was something the owners hadn't had to use before. Towels still had the plastic on them. Males assembled it for sure.

Playtime was over. Sharlee had to get to the office. Calling both a taxi and an Uber when she found a house with the address, she climbed in the taxi because it got to her faster. Competition was the American way.

As Sharlee arrived at the building, she saw Carter standing with the others as the police hauled off Craig Headley and a handful of other men. She walked past Headley as he was swearing they had mistaken him with someone else. He was innocent.

"You! It was you! I'll get you for this! Officer, she's the culprit. She set this all up. I know that's her! That woman is Nona Chance."

The officer sent Craig off with two other officers and approached Sharlee. Jac must have seen her because by the time the officer had stopped beside her, so had the guys.

"Miss Chance?"

"I'm sorry, you have me confused with someone else, I'm afraid. My name is Charlotte Armstrong."

"Do you mind if I see some identification?"

"Not at all, hold on."

Jac slid his arm around her waist.

The officer chuckled. "Know these guys, do you?"

"Yes, I do." She smiled as she handed her driver's license to the officer.

"Thank you, ma'am, I had to check."

"I understand."

Jac pulled her in tightly as the officer nodded in the direction of the assembled men. "Don't worry, Jac, I can see how it is."

Jac nodded in return and led Charlotte upstairs to the offices. As they walked off the elevator, Jac was heading towards the conference room and was met by Mark and Jessie. Mark didn't look too, happy but Jessie was obviously relieved.

"I saw you on the cameras. What happened up here?"

Mark sat Jessie in a seat and got her a bottle of water.

"Geez, Mark, she needs more than that. That maniac's goons were just seconds from finding her."

"Shit." Mark looked hard at Jessie who in turn gave Sharlee an entreating look.

"I could have been wrong. I was under a lot of stress by the man who shoved me inside a steel box!" Sharlee turned her glare to Carter who lifted his hands as if to display his lack of culpability. "Hey, it was a designer steel box. The boss told me to do it. I never disobey a direct order unless the leader is crazy. I happened to think it was a brilliant plan. Except, how did you get out?"

"Yes, Charlotte Hope, how did you get out?" Jac echoed.

"Okay, wait, I have whisky." When she returned and had finished filling the last bathroom size paper cup she said, "This is sipping whiskey, guys. Sipping. Whiskey." She demonstrated by taking a sip of hers and her face broke out in a slow smile. "That's what I'm talking about."

"Charlotte." Jac's tone did not fool anyone. He was being careful because of Jessie.

Sitting up straighter, she began. "Right. So I used the computer in my jail cell to sabotage the guy trying to hack into the office, saw Jessie doing a great job of hiding under her desk from the camera I commandeered, got the police involved and plenty of others. Then I sent my research into my people, a large group I have set up including the newsreels and media. After all of that, getting out of the tin can was easy. We should know what happened to get us in this mess soon. I sent a request to the senator."

"I thought he wasn't answering you," Jac said.

"He is now. I did have to use my real name though, so that's crap. I'm due in his office tomorrow afternoon."

"We are due there tomorrow afternoon."

"Yes, I told him you would say that. He's cool with you tagging along."

Monroe snorted.

Charlotte ignored him and looked over at Jessie. "What happened to everyone? Did they get sent home?"

"Yes." Jessie said quietly not looking up.

"But why were you still here? Did you forget something and get stuck?" Sharlee asked.

Mark turned to the woman seated next to him. "Yes, Jessica Ashlynn, tell us why you were still here after everyone left?"

"Jessica Ashlynn? He knows your middle name? Hot damn girl, you're toast." There was a loud smack. "Ow, Jac."

"Behave."

Sharlee grinned as she rubbed the sting.

"As you were saying?" prompted Mark as he looked at Jessie.

Jessie shrugged. "Um, well, I was working and needed to save my spreadsheets."

Jac grunted and several of the others tried to hide their amusement. Mark had this conversation with them the last time she had stayed too long.

"Jessie, take it from another woman in the middle of this testosterone jungle, just tell it like it is and it will go easier for you."

Mark gave Jessie the look that said he knew she was stalling. "We already know that it saves automatically from the last time you disobeyed a direct order."

"Oh. Well, you were still here." Jessie smirked.

"I was still here because I was preparing to deal with the problem of which you became an integral part."

"I didn't mean to. I was worried about you."

"I appreciate that but now you can worry about yourself."

Leaving that ominous comment on the table, Mark turned to the group. The conversation swung back to the incident earlier in the afternoon. When all the scenarios had been discussed, Mark looked at Jac and around the table.

"So if we're done, I'll get Jessie home."

"Thanks, but I can get myself home." Jessie started to rise from her chair.

"You take the bus."

"So?"

"So you aren't going to do it again. It isn't safe. Say good night. And we won't be in to work tomorrow."

"You don't get to decide how I go home. I'm an adult." Mark ushered Jessie out of the office.

Just as everyone made signs of getting up and going home, Sharlee shook her head. "Jac."

From the hall Jessie shrieked, "Are you kidding me? No way. That's not fair. Mark, it echoes in there!"

Mark's amused chuckling could be heard from the men in the room. "Jac, you can't let Mark spank her."

"I'm not getting in the middle of that." As Sharlee tried to exit his lap, she felt a smack on her thigh again. "And neither are you, baby. You have your own issues to explain."

"What? I did what you told me to do."

"Mostly. Let's head out."

"BUT I DID EVERYTHING you told me to do, and I never even argued with Carter. Well, except when he put me in that tin box jail."

"He did what he could to protect you. On my order."

"I still think he should have told me what was happening."

"Again, on my order, because I knew you would not be okay with being left on the sidelines, even if it was for your own protection."

"Jac, what good is it if I take gun classes, self-defense classes and whatever else you make me do, if I can't use the skills I've learned?"

"Okay, I hear what you're saying but you are my woman. I love you, Charlotte. I'm in love with you, and I do not expose those I love to danger if I can avoid it."

She snuggled into his arms, and he tightened them around her. "I love you too, Jacquard Reynaud, but I don't like not having a say in what happens to me."

"I know. I'm working on that. Give me a chance to get used to our new life in more normal circumstances, okay?"

"Okay. Jac?"

"Hmm?"

"What is your middle name?"

"I don't have one." He reached over and tweaked her nipple under her tank top.

"What? Another thing that is lopsided in your favor? Why no middle name?"

Jac laughed. "I guess so, baby. My parents decided they had done enough of a number on me and I'm thankful. My father liked Maurice."

"Eww, that would have been terrible. Yes, thank goodness."

"Now, I have a need to spank the woman who got out of her safe house before it was safe. The one who has taken so many chances that I have lost count."

"Oh, Jac, can't we just call it good? Compromise?"

"What is the compromise? I spank, you moan, I make love to you."

She slid over his lap and wiggled her bottom enticingly. "What are we waiting for?"

Epilogue

Jac looked at the room and pulled Charlotte onto his lap as he got out his notes. This had been a Charlie Foxtrot, clusterfuck, since it began, and he didn't want to get lost in the tangle of the story. He looked at the men he trusted with his life. The people around this table were important to him. Mark had come in, but Jessie was still home. Evidently, it was Mark's home. He hoped they hit it off for a good long while because she was a damn good accountant.

He began. "Okay, so I think we have figured things out. There are plenty of little connectors we aren't going to make work right now because so much is still being sorted out, but here it is in a nutshell.

"Kyle stole money from a constituent of the senator that we have done work for in the past. He was Craig Headley's boss. The senator told Craig to look into the stolen money and he did. Headley was going to expose Kyle after he wouldn't give him a cut of the profits from the lucrative theft business he had going on. Once Kyle understood the racket Headley had, promises for profit with other countries using the senator's office and name to do it, Kyle offered Charlotte up as a good connection to have because of her skill set. Kyle had no way of knowing what good she would do Headley, but it got him off Kyle's butt."

"I knew he was a weasel," said Kaden.

"That was why I went to Memphis. His mom was there and something he said made me contact his mom. Then something his mom said made it easy to check on things. Kyle had Craig communicate to his mom's shadow email that he monitored. I did the re-routing. It ended up being good evidence for the senator.

"Yes, but that trip was unauthorized and sneaky."

"Jac," said Charlotte.

He ignored her frustration. "However, since Kyle was the one who knew Charlotte, in return for Headley's silence and cover up, he pushed Kyle to hook up with her. When that happened so very easily," Jac stopped to give Charlotte a hard stare, "things were simple."

"Jacquard, it's over, remember? You already sp... we have already discussed this ad nauseam."

Jac nodded and grunted as he patted her leg and held her firmly in his lap. She tried to stand anyway. "So we have, baby." He returned to the conversation, holding her in place.

"The senator already had her on a short list of people they'd vetted and could use in their work. She'd done some minor jobs for him. And we had done several jobs. So, since she was working with us by then, it was easy to access her on several levels. However, the type of work that the senator had intended differed entirely from Headley's work. So when Headley had the camera put in, he found out there already were cameras everywhere."

Garrett grunted. "Bet that was a surprise."

Jac nodded. "One of Charlotte's frequent clients had outside cameras in. We have had a discussion with that client, and he has agreed to never make that mistake again. How he found her is likely from one of the top five guys in her cyber circle. The same one who paid us a visit via our cameras at the end."

Charlotte sat forward and tried to hide a grin when Jac moved her off his cock. "I checked with my group, and it has come out that one of them knew of an operative with skills who had been working with Africa. We are working on getting him exposed. He had to know what he was doing to one of our own. He's going down."

"Then there were our cameras that didn't seem to put either person off when Headley added his own," said Carter.

Charlotte took up the story. "Amateurs. They could have piggy backed the first set and it would have been easier and cleaner. Anyway, then when Craig Headley got the background on who kept coming to my apartment, they used you all to do some work for him, trying another angle. Craig didn't know that you employed me until I showed up with you all at Nnamani's job. He assumed our work was a contract like his. Again, how could he not put that all together?"

Kaden smiled. "Unless he thought you had lots of hunky boyfriends."

Sharlee rolled her eyes.

"He was the one in the window that Charlotte saw. He was doing his best to get us either killed by his goons or discredited for our lack of effectiveness in the securities field. I can only imagine he figured we only played for the home team," Jac added.

"So he was behind that whole mess. The senator's security we handled was also the same senator that Charlotte was doing work for, right?" Garrett was catching on.

"Right. Headley steered the senator to use me multiple times for small jobs and us for security, so it wouldn't feel odd when his office asked me to do a private job for them on a larger scale," Charlotte said.

"Yes, so by the time the conference took place, Charlotte was comfortable working for the senator, and never suspected that there was a problem until she filed a complaint in her report on the second conference," Jac said. "See, the senator hadn't set up that second conference. It was the aide. Until then, Charlotte had occasionally used a broker for the jobs. So when Headley misrepresented himself on the contract set up, she had no idea. She thought it was the same broker, and she simply didn't use him any longer. The mix up diverted her from the actual path long enough for the last office breach."

"I think I see where this is going. Sharlee became an extra at that point. It was obvious she wasn't as easy to manipulate as Craig Headley and his cronies had hoped and when they tried to set her up for the fall, like following her, the apartment break-ins, the office break-ins, and probably other things, all those were to frame her somehow for the actions they were doing. They were trying to get to her points of access so they could plant information and point the finger at her. She would have taken the fall," Monroe pieced together.

"I get it now," said Garrett. "He knew if they couldn't find a way to discredit her and stop her, she would eventually figure out that they had done illegal things. I bet he was frantic, thinking she was going to put the pieces together any day."

Jac nodded his head. "You're partly right. And if we weren't so busy, she would have done it. It would have been a piece of cake for Charlotte to manipulate the whole outcome and flip it on him. But it wasn't about only discrediting her, it was about using her."

"Yes, but why?" Carter asked.

"Trafficking drugs and women, according to the senator's investigations," answered Charlotte.

"So we were supposed to be pawns until they decided we weren't easily manipulated and then they needed to dispose of Charlotte. The senator believes they wanted to discredit her, set her up in a blackmail situation so that she would change sides, so to speak, and work for them. With Charlotte on their side, the heavens would open up for them. When it didn't work, they had to kill her, but we had taken over her protection by then." Jac looked at his woman. "Even though she made it difficult at times to do our job, it was good enough."

"Again, discussed and moved on," she said with a shake of her head.

"So our man Kyle had outlived his usefulness pretty early on I guess. They had him arrested," Kaden said.

"Yep, and set him up pretty easily. That was when Kyle realized that he wasn't just in a small group of cons, but in the high stakes game and hence the warning to me as they were taking him away. He also knew my real name."

"Yep, and Kyle sang long and loud. The senator was watching for what had happened next," said Jac.

"Wait, the senator already knew about Headley?" demanded Mark, who had been quiet until this point.

"Yes," Sharlee said. "Or suspected him anyway."

"And just when was he going to stop him—after he had taken care of you?" Mark was mad. He had been in a strong protective mode since Jessie had entered the picture more prominently. It spilled over heavily to Sharlee.

"He was just piecing it all together, but he might have been too slow to believe his top aide was that corrupt, a notch above even for Washington," Jac said as he tightened his hold on the woman in his lap.

Monroe leaned back and said. "So that's it."

"Yep, that's it," said Jac leaning back in his chair.

"Hey, no, that isn't it. Remember that stupid, moronic bet you guys had about me and the Christmas party this year?" Moans could be heard throughout the room. "Yes, I can see you do. Well because of you boys, I dated Kyle, signed up for a dating service," she held up her hand, "me in pseudo form, and spoke to all manner of men trying to get a date. Then I chased Jac. Finally, I got Jac, and he is taking me to the party, but you all caused part of our collective trouble this year so, if you don't mind, I'll take the betting pot and go buy a nice dress and if there is enough, shoes."

Carter spoke up. "You haven't shown up with a date yet."

"Do you really think that Jacquard would dare stand me up?"

"Pay up boys, she won," said Jac with a laugh.

"Both bets." Charlotte reminded them.

The men complained and grumbled but laughed.

Monroe said, "But Jac didn't even bet."

"You forget, I wanted to take her and would never bet against myself. Besides, I'll be paying for everything the winnings don't cover." Charlotte kissed his cheek.

"Now are we done?" asked Mark.

"Yes, now we are done."

"Good." Mark got up. "I say we all take a week off and discover what normal is like again."

"Wait, no, I have a question first." Charlotte sat up and gave everyone in the room an irritated stare.

"If you must," Carter said sarcastically.

Sharlee threw a pen at him that he caught in one hand.

"Nice, man," Kaden slapped Carter on the back. Carter grinned and shrugged.

"No, what about that room you made Carter shove me into?"

Jac looked as though it were obvious. "Safe room. I think I'm going to build an entire building over it."

"It's in a neighborhood, Jac."

"Best place to hide, in the middle of people."

"But it isn't zoned for business."

"I'm learning a little from the woman with multiple aliases."

"Hey, yeah, what's up with that, Char, I mean 'Ms. Chance'?" Kaden asked with a grin on his face.

"Charlotte, you moron. And a woman needs some secrets." She turned back to Jac. "Well if we're keeping the classy steel box, I have some technology suggestions, and who was your decorator?"

LYING IN BED, SATIATED, Charlotte sighed with happiness. "It was a good idea to close the office for a week."

"Yes and I know what I'm going to do with this next week," said Jac.

"Wait, Jac. Are we really done with all this crazy business?" asked Charlotte.

"Other than your testimony, yes, we are all done."

"Good because I want to take on a new contract when our week is over." Charlotte wiggled in excitement.

"We'll talk about it."

"Wait, now, I'm an adult and I have a business. I don't tell you which jobs you should take."

"I see, so you pay taxes on this business," asked Jac with raised eyebrows.

"Oh, well, um, probably."

Jac laughed, "You should know if you do or don't pay taxes."

Charlotte rolled onto her side to cuddle in more. "Do you think Jessie is all right?"

"Nice subject change, young lady and yes. I think she's going to be fine."

"Mark spanked her, you know."

"No, I didn't know, but I don't disapprove. Jessie is going to need to learn to follow his orders when he's trying to keep her safe or she'll find herself with a hot butt often. Just like someone else I know."

"I'm better," said Sharlee smugly.

He snorted. "If you say so, baby."

"Well, I'm trying."

"Yes, you are but could you try a little harder? I have a feeling the female population is going to increase in our office in the next few years and we need to finish training one brat before we get another."

She clamped her hand tightly onto his member. "Hmm, I'll show you bratty."

He slapped her upturned left ass cheek. "And I'll show you discipline."

She shivered and whimpered.

"Or I could show you something we'll both like."

Charlotte loosened her hand and rolled on top of Jac. Lowering her lips to his she whispered, "Yes, please."

The End

About the Author

Alyssa Bailey

USA Today Bestselling Author of Sassy Romance that is realistic and sensual with a touch of suspense. A dyed-in-the-wool Texan living in Alaska for half her life, Alyssa now divides her time between the beauty of Southeast Alaska and the Piney Woods of Northeast Texas. She enjoys taking from her own experiences to create series in fictitious worlds sure to tease the reader's palate and invite them to sink into exciting adventures.

Alyssa enjoys writing consensual power exchanges between intelligent, sassy women who are not afraid to make a stand and loving men confident enough to give their woman space but masterful enough to keep her indulged and protected. There is *always* a "happily ever after."

Visit me online and sign up for my Newsletter:

Connect with Alyssa Bailey: alyssabailey.com/

Other Books By Alyssa Bailey

Safe and Secure Series: Contemporary, suspense, spicy
Saving Sharlee
Saving Jessie (re-release 2023)
Saving Ivy
Saving Mallory
Saving Callie
Saving Becky
Saving Finley (2023)

CLEARWATER RANCH TRILOGY -Contemporary, Spicy
Piper's Plan (re-release 2024)
Camille's Second Chance (re-release 2024)
Josie's Refuge

DARLING DUCHESSES: Regency, Daddy Dom, Spicy
The Devil Duke's Little Distraction
The Daring Duke's Little Impulse

GUARDIANS OF REFUGE (Contemporary, Military, Spicy)
    SEAL of Refuge
    The Strategy of Love
    The Tactics of Love
    The Mandate of Love

SAGE COUNTY (Cowboy, Contemporary, Spicy)
    Deep Waters
    Still Waters

IN THE SPIRIT OF CHRISTMAS -Contemporary, Sweet
    Christmas Wishes and You

ANTHOLOGIES (HEAT VARIES)
    Sweet Town Love
    Historical Heroes
    Hero to Obey (limited time)
    Cowboy for a Cause (limited time)
    Naughty 12 Days of Christmas 2017

MULTI-AUTHOR BOX SETS (Heat Level Various)
    Love, Christmas 2 Recipes
    Irresistible Heroes
    Sweet and Sassy Summertime Vol. 2

Dear Santa: A Christmas Wish
Sweet and Sassy New Beginnings

Audiobooks
Accepting His Ways
Her Sweet Complication
His Gentle Persuasion
Quinlan's Quest
Lady Caroline's Defiance

These books will be re-released soon...

Lords and Little Ladies: Georgian Historical, spicy
Lord Thayer's Choice
Lord Ashton's Decision
The Black Laird Requires
Lord Kendrick's Obligation

CHASE ABBEY SERIES: Regency, Spicy, Suspense
Lord Barrington's Minx
Becoming Lady Barrington
Lady Caroline's Defiance
His Improper Lady

THE O'CONNOR SERIES: Contemporary, Rancher, Saga, Spicy
Liam & Jocelyn's Story
Her Sweet Complication
Liam's Lessons
Loving Liam

CIARÁN AND KATHERINE'S Story
His Gentle Persuasion
Rancher's Creed
Katie Consents

QUINLAN AND CHEYENNE'S Story
Quinlan's Quest
Accepting His Way
Her Balancing Act

KELLI AND PARKER'S Story
Meeting Her Needs
Kissing Kelli
Keeping Kelli

CIÁN AND MOLLY'S STORY
In Pursuit of Molly
Freeing Molly
Forever Molly

LONE WIND SERIES: Contemporary, spicy Native American
Reclaiming Clover

TAMING TEXANNA -American Historical, Native American, Spicy

    Cowboy Welcome- Contemporary, Spicy

Alyssa Bailey written as Tasha Winters

To Be Re-Released Soon...

CAPTURED SERIES-URBAN Fantasy/Time Travel
Captured Obedience
Captured Desire

ALPHAS IN THE WILD
Wild Alpha Fantasy
Wild Alpha Promise

Don't miss out!

Visit the website below and you can sign up to receive emails whenever Alyssa Bailey publishes a new book. There's no charge and no obligation.

https://books2read.com/r/B-A-MXIL-CPUIC

BOOKS2READ

Connecting independent readers to independent writers.

Did you love *Saving Sharlee*? Then you should read *Saving Callie* by Alyssa Bailey!

Loyalty is good, but blind loyalty is deadly.

Garrett Sullivan and Katrina Long, known as Callie to Garrett and friends due to her California beach upbringing was in a serious dating arrangement. He loved her. They argued over her taking an undercover job with Homeland Security into the dark underworld of the Mexican Mafia in Southern California. The next evening there was a note from Callie saying her dad was sick and she'd call when she got there. She never called.

After a year of pounding her family and Homeland for information where his girl was, his team found her but she slipped away when approached. Soon afterwards Garrett was told she was dead but he never believed it. Now, three years later, Sharlee received a call from Callie who was in trouble but disconnected before Sharlee could trace her. Garrett's primary goal was to get Callie to safety and after that, he didn't know.

Within a week, Homeland wanted him to lead a team for a local job two years after Callie's old employers had tried hard to distance themselves from him. Something fishy was going on and Garrett and teammates would figure it out but in the meantime, they would find and save Callie from whatever danger she was in before it was too late.

Read more at alyssabailey.com.

Also by Alyssa Bailey

Safe and Secure
Saving Sharlee

Watch for more at alyssabailey.com.

www.ingramcontent.com/pod-product-compliance
Lightning Source LLC
Chambersburg PA
CBHW071851220626
47052CB00002B/71